23 Miles

Renee MacKenzie

Affinity
eBook Press
NZ
2015

23 Miles

© by Renee MacKenzie 2015

Affinity E-Book Press NZ LTD
Canterbury, New Zealand

1st Edition

ISBN: 978-1-927328-52-1

This is a work of fiction. Names, character, places, and incidents are the product of the author's imagination or are used fictitiously and any resemblance to actual persons living or dead, businesses, companies, events, or locales is entirely coincidental.

Editor: Ruth Stanley
Proof Editor: Alexis Smith
Cover Design: Irish Dragon Designs

Acknowledgments

Big thanks go out to my publishing family at Affinity E-Books Press NZ—Julie for having faith in my work; to Mel for her awesome formatting; to Ruth for the exceptional edit; Nancy for the incredible cover; Kay for being my beta reader extraordinaire, and Robin for her great promotion.

A very special thank-you to Bill Thomas for so graciously talking to me about the loss of his beloved sister, Cathy. He is truly an inspiration and I am happy to count him as a friend. Every time I thought I'd walk away from this project, even if just for a break, I thought of Bill and knew I had to keep at it.

And to my family—thanks to Pam Bauserman for her love and support and patience (and that's a lot of patience). I love you more each and every day, Pam. To Carol, Candy, Stacey, and Kemp, thanks for always being there, being supportive, and for being willing to call me out when necessary. I know I don't say it nearly enough, but I love you all.

Thanks to Annette, Chris, Lyndon, Karla, and so many others who talked to me about the cases on the parkway, although they would rather forget, and felt less than comfortable talking about that painful time.

Thanks to my sister-in-law, Monica Bauserman, for being my biggest cheerleader through all of my novels. Karin Gillespie, Steve Fox, and Christine Clark gave invaluable feedback as my first readers. Thanks Kemp MacKenzie for 'Liarhead Lizard' all those years ago.

To my family at the Hershee Bar—thank you for being there for me and everyone else for over thirty years. Annette and Bill, you were such a huge influence on so many of us as we found our way. I love you both.

I would like to acknowledge prior publication of "Taste" and "Soul Dancing" (published as "Heady Dancing") in the 1998 issue of *Sandhills Magazine*, and "No" in the 1999 issue of that magazine.

Dedication

For the victims and their families—may you receive justice and find peace.

Table of Contents

Also by Renee MacKenzie

Nesting
Confined Spaces
Flight

Chapter One

October 1986

Shay Eliot pulled her Chevy C10 pickup truck into a parking space close to the entrance of the bar. There were only a few other cars in the lot. She turned off the ignition and leaned her head back. She had been to this bar hundreds of times—first as just a patron, then as Dee's friend, and then as a law enforcement officer.

There weren't a lot of problems at the bar. The fact that Dee would ban you for life for fighting did a lot to deter that kind of trouble. Usually the only problems were an occasional local punk yelling anti-gay rhetoric or the sporadic lover's quarrel that would lead to sloppy breakups that only lasted until the following weekend.

Shay took a deep breath and let it out slowly. She would continue coming to the bar as a patron and a friend, but never again as a law enforcement officer.

"What have I done?" she whispered. It started to drizzle again and she stared through the spotted and streaked windshield at the building's painted cinderblock.

When she got out of the truck, she gave the parking lot a quick, visual scan. Her attention came to rest on the far right corner of the building where two bowls were set off to the side. It appeared Lana, or one of the other bartenders, had taken to feeding the feral cat that had started hanging around. Shay chuckled because she had known Dee's 'no strays' rule wouldn't last the week.

Here goes. She pulled the heavy door open and stopped just inside, waiting for her eyes to adjust to the darker interior. A woman leaning against the cigarette machine smiled at her. Shay nodded.

"I did it," Shay blurted out to Lana Christianson as she sat at the bar.

"You did what and what'll you have?" Lana asked as she adjusted her long, dark ponytail and reached for a glass hanging from the rack above her head.

"A vodka tonic and make it a double." Shay swiveled around looking at the few people in the bar at that early hour. "Oh, and a shot of tequila."

Phil Collins crooned "One More Night" from the jukebox. Shay much preferred his songs to the dance music that inevitably would take over later. She watched two women chalk up their pool cues as they eyed each other across the green felt table. Shay found their game of psych-out amusing. Running her hand over her semi-short, wavy hair, she watched them stare each other down.

Lana set Shay's drink in front of her, and then poured the shot. As Shay reached for the tequila, Lana placed her hand over Shay's and the shot. "Whoa," she said. Shay could tell Lana was nervous, probably because she'd never seen Shay do shots before.

Lana's voice lowered to a near-whisper. "What did you do?"

"I quit the force." She slid the shot out from under Lana's hand, held it up for a salute, slipped the lemon slice off the rim, and downed the shot. She ignored the saltshaker Lana slid in her direction and stuck the lemon into her mouth.

"You...did...what?" Lana's voice rose with each word.

Shay put the lemon slice in the empty shot glass. "I quit my job."

Shay had talked to Lana a couple of times about a rough patch she was going through at work. She told her about how she hadn't been considered for a promotion in years, about how she always felt a little on the outside at work.

"I thought it was all just you venting," Lana said. She wiped the bar around Shay and then emptied a nearby ashtray.

Shay studied Lana's face. "Well, aren't you going to say anything else?"

The door to the back cooler swung open. "Lana, can you help me with this keg?" Dee fumbled with the heavy keg as she tried to roll it out of the cooler. The bar manager's skinny arms were all angles and elbows.

"I got it," Shay said. "Might as well make myself useful before I'm too drunk to be any good to anyone."

Dee gave Lana a what's-up look. Shay wasn't worried, knowing Lana wouldn't say anything until Shay was ready for the world to know. Out of the corner of her eye she saw Lana shake her head before following Shay to the keg.

Shay maneuvered the keg into place and set it up. She felt both Lana and Dee watching her so she flexed her muscles an extra little bit. She wasn't necessarily vain, but she worked hard to stay fit and liked it when people expressed appreciation for her physique. She hooked the keg up for Dee, something she'd done many times over the years.

Before Shay could sit down, Lana grabbed her by the hand and led her out the door to the parking lot. She didn't stop until they were a good distance from the door.

"Tell me exactly what you did."

Shay crossed her arms over her chest. "I quit my job with the police department." She waited a beat before saying, "Oh, you mean *exactly* what I did. Well, what I *meant* to do was walk in, hand that asshole sergeant of mine my badge and service revolver, and say screw you." She took a deep breath. "But the reality of it was a little different. The sergeant wouldn't take my badge or gun. He sent me to human resources where I very civilly signed my paperwork. Then they sent me to property and accounting so I could give them my belt, uniforms, badge, and gun."

"Why?" Lana asked.

"Why property and accounting?" Shay asked, knowing she was bordering on being obnoxious.

"No, why quit the force?"

3

"My loyalty is to my community, not my employers, and that's not acceptable, not to them and not to me." Shay knew it sounded rehearsed but didn't care.

"Did you quit because of that thing with Paulie? Oh my God, Shay, you didn't, did you?"

"You know how much that whole thing sickened me," she said as she used her foot to scoot some gravel around on the pavement.

"Shay, we don't even know if Paulie was telling the truth. What if he was lying? You threw it all away over him?"

"We'll probably never know the truth about that night. Maybe Paulie did resist arrest. Or maybe my brothers in blue— " Shay stopped, almost choking on the words. "Maybe Dixon and McCoy did beat the shit out of 'the little fag boy' for no reason."

"So why quit if you don't even know who to believe?" Lana asked.

"*Because* I don't know who to believe. I should have total faith in my fellow officers, but I don't. I've heard enough fag jokes out of them to last a lifetime. The worst part—the very worst part—was how my sergeant not only blew off my concerns about the assault on Paulie, but ridiculed me over them in front of the others. When I looked around the squad room and didn't definitively believe they had my back…" She stopped to compose herself. "…I knew I couldn't be there anymore."

Lana reached for her, but stopped. "Wow," she whispered. "Just…wow."

As a car pulled into the parking lot, illuminating them with its headlights, Shay said, "We should go in."

"Yeah."

Back inside, Lana resumed her duties, serving the women on the left side of the bar while Dee concentrated on those on the right.

After Shay downed another shot and two doubles, Lana placed a plain Coke on the bar in front of her.

"I'm such a lightweight. And you know me so well," Shay joked.

"It's my job to know when it's soda time." She reached into the sink and started washing glasses as she spoke to Shay. "Does Kate know you were going to quit your job?"

"No. You're the only one I've talked to about the Paulie thing and, other than a softball buddy, the only one I've told so far about quitting." Shay fidgeted with her glass and thought about the first time she'd met Kate and Lana. Shay was one of the first cops at a crime scene in which Kate was suspected of murdering Lana's boyfriend, Richie. By the end of the case, Shay was left with a mad crush on Kate, who hadn't murdered anyone, a friend in Lana, and now, three years later, no career.

"When's your girl coming in?" Shay asked, trying to shake off her thoughts.

Lana's face reddened at her words. Shay smiled. She liked that Lana still reacted that way to the mention of Kate. It was no secret in their little piece of the world that Shay'd had a bit of a crush on Kate when they first met.

"She's going to study sociopaths and psychopaths until she's half-blind, then she'll come by for a little while. So, probably not until midnight or later." Lana sighed.

Shay was glad that Kate and Lana had worked through their issues from three years earlier when Lana was having trouble inching her way out of the closet and gave into pressure from her mother to go straight. Shay just wanted Kate to be happy. She watched Lana serving drinks, and was glad to have helped her get the job there and an apartment nearby. Shay still wasn't sure if Lana would have been able to resist her family's demands concerning her sexuality if she hadn't put a little distance between them.

"If you don't mind, would you tell Kate about me quitting?" Shay asked, recognizing that she used Lana as a buffer between her and Kate.

"Don't you think that should come from you?"

"No. I'd rather you tell her, then I can fill in details later for her. I can hear her now, '*Eliot, why would you let them run you off from doing what you love?*'"

"And your response would be?"

Shay shrugged. "She's the only person outside of work who calls me Eliot," she said, not caring that she was going off topic.

"Because for the longest time she only knew you as S. Eliot from your name tag. Calling you S. was a little weird for her."

Shay laughed. "It sounds sweet when she says it. Not like when my sergeant growls it out." Shay shut up then, afraid her torch might be showing.

"What are you going to do for work?"

"My friend Brenda set me up with a few yards to mow. It's not much, but it's something." Shay had been thankful that her softball buddy had such a successful lawn business that she could throw a little work her way. But she wasn't sure how long that would be enough, both mentally and financially. She had a good-sized nest egg built up, thanks to her parents drilling into her head the importance of saving for a rainy day, but she knew it wouldn't hold up forever.

†

Talia Lisher sang at the top of her lungs to Sam Harris's "Sugar Don't Bite" as she drove her 1982 Honda Accord to the Colonial Parkway. The twenty-three mile scenic roadway that connected Yorktown, Williamsburg, and Jamestown was the preferred spot for partying for many of her old high school friends. Talia was looking for Fish, the dude she got her pot from. A few minutes later, she pulled off the parkway near Yorktown, into a scenic overview. As if on cue, Fish pulled in right behind her. She'd recognize his Dodge Challenger anywhere. They both killed their headlights, then Fish got into her car and they smoked a joint before Talia bought a nickel bag from him.

Pulling out of the scenic overview, her mouth was dry—cottonmouth from smoking the weed—and she craved a Slim Jim and potato chips, her version of a meat and potatoes diet. She'd wash it down with an ice-cold Jolt Cola, getting just the desired kick so she could sit down and scratch out a poem or two.

She noted yellows and oranges dotting the trees as autumn's display of colors started. The yellows in particular glowed in the beam of her headlights. This was her favorite time of year. She loved the changing colors of the foliage, and she liked being able to wear her funky-patterned blazers out to the bar without getting too warm in them.

When Talia passed the pull-off near Ringfield Park, a dark van pulled out behind her. It sped up until it was right on the bumper of her Honda. She increased her speed, and so did the dark van. She couldn't tell if it was black or dark blue; she only knew it was too close for comfort.

What if it's the cops? she wondered in her marijuana-induced paranoia. No, no way they'd be out here in a van. Besides, she was on federal land. It'd be the park service rangers patrolling there, not the state or county. Right?

Talia turned the music way down, as if to help her concentrate on driving. She sped up further but the van stayed right on her. The buzz she'd worked so hard to get disappeared and fear took over.

The van flashed its lights like it wanted her to stop. She felt a little sick. Again it flashed its lights— off and on, off and on, low beams to high beams. Then the inside of her car lit up with what she assumed was a spotlight. A voice screaming in her head told her if she stopped, she'd be dead.

She stomped on the accelerator and didn't ease up, not even around the tree-lined curves. The van stayed with her at first, but by the third time she took a curve on two wheels, she had pulled way ahead of it. She didn't let up.

She meant to get off the parkway at Route 17, but was going too fast by the time she approached. She would have to go to Ballard Street.

The stop sign at the intersection with Ballard came out of nowhere. She slowed just enough to turn right without losing control. There were no headlights behind her. She turned right onto Cook Road and kept her speed at the limit, not wanting to draw attention to herself and not wanting to hit a deer. Good thing she hadn't seen any deer on the parkway. The way she was driving there would have been no way to avoid one.

Once Talia had backtracked and was finally on Route 17 she felt a little safer. She glanced into the rearview mirror every few moments as she wove her way to the intersection of Ft. Eustis Boulevard and Jefferson Avenue. She knew she wouldn't be able to keep food down, so she didn't stop at the 7-Eleven. Several minutes later she pulled into the parking lot of her apartment and looked around. Not seeing a dark van, she got out, locked the car behind her, and ran to her apartment door.

Once inside, she locked the door and threw the dead bolt, and then went into the kitchen and pulled out an Amstel Light. She took several gulps. She didn't like beer, but bought it when she saw Shay Eliot drinking that brand at the bar one night after her shift as a law enforcement officer.

Talia went into the bathroom and looked in the mirror. She cringed at the amount of mascara smeared under her eyes, her purple eye shadow was mostly gone, her "big hair" was way too massive, and she was pale. She looked like a vampire. And she was still shaking from the chase on the parkway.

"What the hell was that about?" she asked her reflection.

She went into the living room and grabbed the phone off the side table, stretching the cord out as far as it would go as she sat on the sofa. Dialing her best friend's phone number in Georgia, she wished Debbie hadn't left Virginia. If Debbie had stayed instead of moving, they would have been cruising the parkway together. But her best friend had left the area, was oblivious to where Talia spent her time now, and pretty much had started growing further and further from her. Talia knew she was lying by omission to Debbie by not coming out to her, but she could live with that.

"You will not believe what happened to me," Talia said in lieu of hello.

"Talia? It's late. I've got class tomorrow."

"Oh, sorry, but I have to tell you what happened. I was on the parkway. I'd just scored some weed from Fish—"

"You're still smoking that trash from Fish?"

"Hey, things have been dry lately. I take what I can get, you know?" She took a sip of her beer. "So, listen, I'm driving home and all of a sudden this dark van pulls up behind me and is right on my ass. And he chases me. He's flashing his lights and shining some spotlight on me and won't back off."

"Just some jerk-off messing with you," Debbie mumbled.

Talia felt a surge of energy move through her. *Just some jerk-off?* Really? She couldn't believe she was inches from death and her best friend was blowing her off.

She felt it coming, but was powerless against it. "Debbie, he hit me from behind," she lied.

"What?"

There, now I have your attention. "Well, it was only a tap, and it didn't do any damage, but I came really close to losing control of the car and we were going like seventy on that one curving section of the parkway."

"Shit, you need to stay away from there for a while. What if it was someone who knew you'd scored some weed and was going to roll you for it?"

"*Roll me for it?* Where in the world did you pick up that jargon?"

Debbie laughed. "Too much cable TV, I suppose. Still, you need to be careful."

Talia sat back, snuggling into the sofa, feeling better now that her best friend was showing a more appropriate level of concern.

†

Shay rolled over and looked at the clock on the bedside table. Her tabby cat, Poke, was at the foot of the bed, meowing. "Come up here, brat," she told him, patting her stomach. He climbed onto her and she petted his gray, brown, and black head. "Thanks for still loving me even if I probably won't be able to afford cat treats for too much longer."

He jumped off her and she laughed. "Yeah, I see how you are."

Mornings were the hardest time of the day. It was when she was most likely to examine the place she was at in her life. Sighing, she looked at the clock again. She would have to get up soon if she was going to finish all the lawns on her schedule for the day. She was so glad Brenda had given her a few clients while she was starting out. Brenda was always so busy that she wouldn't even feel the effect. But it sure would help Shay.

Shay's head pounded as she made her way to the bathroom. What was she thinking drinking shots of tequila? Oh, that's right, she *hadn't* been thinking.

She threw on an old pair of jeans and a T-shirt, and then made her way into the kitchen. She poured herself a bowl of Corn Flakes. Poke eyed her. Shay was pretty sure he was convinced that she went without milk in her cereal to torture him. "Sorry, buddy," she said as she poured herself a glass of orange juice and stood at the kitchen counter to eat her dry cereal.

She freshened Poke's water and kibble, then brushed her teeth and started out the door. She stopped short at the edge of the driveway and wondered how long it would take before she grew used to not seeing her police cruiser there.

She checked the time and knew she'd better get going if she was going to get all the lawns done in time to beat the navy base traffic. She checked that the lawnmower was secured in the back of her Chevy C10 pickup truck, jiggled the gas can to be sure she had enough diesel fuel to mow several lawns with her old, commercial mower, and then was on her way.

✝

Talia came home from her job at the dental office one town over, in Grafton, and threw the bag of Taco Bell on the table. She grabbed a Jolt Cola from the fridge and settled down to eat her tostada and two tacos. *Thank God for Taco Bell.* It was her usual Thursday night cuisine. And Tuesday, Wednesday, and sometimes Sunday. "Okay," she admitted to herself. "I'm addicted."

She squirted some hot sauce onto her taco and thought about the crappy day she'd had at work. She had a hell of a time finding the right balance of caffeine to wake up but not be jittery. She couldn't get in a groove and felt like Dr. Bennett was waiting on her for one thing or another all day. A couple of times she'd glanced toward Lacey, the other dental assistant, and caught her making faces behind the dentist's back. Lacey was always good for comic relief. Talia thought Lacey was nice to her because her presence there took the pressure off her. She was pretty sure Lacey was the recipient of all the impatience before Talia joined the office.

Sauce dripped down Talia's chin as she devoured her second taco. She swiped carelessly at it with a napkin.

Earlier, at the office, she'd been wiping down the handles of the light over the dental chair and looked up to see Dr. Bennett standing in the doorway with a patient. Dr. Bennett gripped the patient's chart to his chest. Talia wasn't sure if she'd zoned out and spent way too long cleaning, or if he was just giving her the look he used often to remind her not to think too much of herself. And every time she looked toward the front of the office she noticed Sally, the receptionist, looking at her accusingly.

To make matters worse, Talia couldn't shake the discomfort lingering after her encounter on the parkway the night before. Every time she thought about it her heart pounded and she felt a little sick. She decided to think of it as a sign that she was meant to stay home more nights. She should be working on her poetry chapbook after work, not being chased down by some freak up to God knows what. But she could still go to the bar on the other side of the Hampton Roads Bridge-Tunnel in Norfolk and try to talk to Shay Eliot, of course.

Standing in her apartment's small hallway, she looked toward the poem room, as she called it. It was meant to be Brian's room when he got out of prison, but with a minimum of four years left on her brother's sentence, Talia could still call it whatever she wanted to for quite some time. And she'd be lying—which she'd been working hard at lately to quit—if she didn't admit that she would rather Brian not move in with her when he got out. Drama followed Brian, and Talia wasn't a big fan of drama. Then there was the whole gay thing. She instinctively knew she would always need to hide that part of her life from her brother.

So, the poem room... Talia had painted a poem on a canvas two days earlier. It was one inspired by a dream she had about Shay Eliot. She'd titled it, "Soul Dancing."

11

Talia had this process where she painted a 24 x 36-inch canvas with acrylic paints. One color, kind of light, covered the entire surface, then she painted on the words, large and bold. It was something new she'd started. So far, other than the dancing poem, she also had "Taste" (also inspired by Shay Eliot), "No," and "Under the Ball Cap." It was sort of her thing. Every writer needed a thing, she'd decided.

After finishing her dinner, she went into the poem room. "Soul Dancing" was written in bold black letters scratched onto a steel-blue background that reminded her of the color of Shay Eliot's eyes. Talia was going through a phase where she wasn't allowing her poems to rhyme. She'd heard that was what the cool writers were doing.

The canvas leaned on the easel where she'd left it to dry. She stood in front of it and stared until the light blue background turned into Shay Eliot's eyes. Then she began reciting it, mostly from memory.

"On that day when
strong women
are invited to dance
barefoot in my dust,
I know
you will be there,
beautiful feet glistening
with life's sheen.
My barefoot Muse,
set free my obsession,
take me with you and
leave a trail of me.
Help me to know what you view,
to see what you know,
strong woman
barefoot in my dust."

Talia loved writing but knew she wasn't going to make a living at it. She liked working as a dental assistant just fine, but didn't want to do it forever. Other than writing poems, she didn't know what else she was interested in. She figured maybe she'd work that out by the time she burned out on the dental assistant gig. She had just turned twenty-three, made a decent wage, loved the car Brian sold to her for ten bucks before being sent away, and liked her apartment in Newport News fine, even if she would have preferred to stay in York County.

The only thing she found lacking was her sex life. After fooling around a bit when she first came out, she hadn't been with anyone in a while. She knew that was her own fault for holding out for the woman of her dreams. Speaking of whom, she wondered if Shay Eliot was at the bar. She could go see. No, she reminded herself. It was poem night—even if it meant staring at the walls or ceiling while waiting for her muse.

The phone rang. Thursday was also the day Brian got his phone time. She picked up the receiver. "Yes, I'll accept the charges," she responded to the operator's inquiry.

Chapter Two

It was Friday night and Talia was ready to party. She bypassed a closer parking spot behind the bar in Norfolk to park further away, next to Shay Eliot's tan pickup truck. She wished she had a shot of something to take the edge off, but hadn't replaced the schnapps under the front seat after she'd finished it a few nights earlier. Tonight, after a few drinks, she was going to finally get the courage up to approach Shay and say hello. That was the plan.

She could smell the aroma of pot coming from a partially opened car window and wished she was bold enough to approach and ask for a hit. But she wasn't. She wished she had brought her own instead of leaving it stashed at home.

Talia showed Cindy, the woman at the door, her ID and stepped into the smoky bar. Several women were shooting pool in the area right inside the door. Talia glanced around, looking for Shay.

It didn't take long for Talia to find her, sitting at the bar, talking to a bartender. Talia checked out the cute bartender, Lana. She'd figured out that Lana was dating Kate Hunter, a girl Talia knew from high school. Just then, Kate walked up to the bar from the direction of the restrooms and sat down next to Shay.

Not for the first time, Talia saw the way Shay looked at Kate, causing Talia to cringe. She wondered if there was ever anything there.

Talia tucked herself near the jukebox where she could watch Shay from a distance. She ordered a greyhound from the waitress, then changed her mind and went with a vodka tonic. She needed to stay away from the grapefruit juice because of its acidity, and because she didn't like the taste in her mouth by the end of the night when she drank it. She assumed it didn't smell that great to people she wanted to impress either. And by people she meant Shay.

The jukebox grew quiet and a DJ started playing. The music started off with some new Janet Jackson—"Control" followed by "Nasty." Talia liked the sound and was a little disappointed when the DJ switched it up and played "I Fall to Pieces." But the DJ got Talia's attention when she dedicated it to Shay.

Talia thought it a peculiar choice, old-fashioned and not very danceable, but noticed the smile on Shay's face as it played. She made a mental note to get a cassette of Patsy Cline as soon as she could.

"The women of *Dynasty* called. They want their shoulder pads back," a voice behind Talia said.

Talia gave the shoulders of her black and gray paisley jacket a slight adjustment, and then made sure the collar was flipped up with the appropriate level of coolness. "You're just jealous, Beth."

Beth smiled and stared at her a moment longer than what was comfortable. "Damn, girl, you look beat."

She wasn't about to tell Beth that hanging out at the bar almost every night was wearing her out. Talia shrugged, then regretted drawing Beth's attention back to the butt of her joke. "What's up?"

"I am." Beth laughed.

"Oh?"

"Buy me a drink and I'll give you a robin egg."

Talia considered the diet pills she liked to use for a rush and that I'm-so-euphoric feeling. "How about two robin eggs?" Talia asked.

"I forget it takes a lot to get you off."

Talia was caught a little off guard by the comment, but tried to play it off. "Who's been talking?" she teased.

"I didn't mean it like that. But now that you ask, Lori's been lamenting how you were a much better lay than Chris and she should have stayed with you."

"I told her she'd be missing me," Talia said, bragging with more confidence than she really felt. Lori was a woman she'd met shortly after finding her way to the lesbian bar in Norfolk. Talia had slept with her when she first came out to the bar. She liked Lori, liked her a lot, but so did their mutual friend, Chris.

"Do you and your shoulder pads want to dance?" Beth asked.

"Only if you quit with the fashion judgment."

Talia was a decent dancer and held her own through a Madonna song and one by Prince. She was pretty sure after a few more drinks she'd think she was a dancing goddess. She watched Beth, who was a good dancer, fluid and graceful.

Talia glanced into the floor-to-ceiling mirror at the back of the dance floor to check on her hair. She always blew it out for extra height when going out to the bar. Satisfied with it, she turned back to Beth and concentrated on letting the music wash over her.

Cyndi Lauper came on as Talia looked over Beth's shoulder and saw Shay was still at the bar talking to Kate. "Let's get your drink," she said as she led Beth off the dance floor.

Talia stepped to the bar and ordered. When she handed Beth her drink, Beth slipped two pills into Talia's front pocket, her fingers lingering there a few moments longer than necessary. Talia glanced at Shay to make sure she hadn't seen.

Once out of Shay's line of sight, Talia washed down one of the pills with her cocktail. She wanted to save the other for right before she left to drive home. The forty-minute drive was always a little easier with some speed in her.

Beth took off to hang out with some softball pals of hers. Talia continued to watch Shay at the bar, thinking that at any second she'd get up the nerve to talk to her.

Talia wished Kate would go away. Kate was never rude, and didn't pretend not to know Talia, but she wasn't actually friendly either. And Talia sure as hell wouldn't go up to talk to Shay with Kate sitting right there.

Talia let her mind wander back to the first time she'd seen Shay Eliot. It was a Friday night and Shay was the cop responding to the break-in of a car in the parking lot at the bar. When she walked inside, all heads turned to look at her, including Talia's. Shay nodded with familiarity at several of the patrons, and then went up to the bar to talk to Dee, who was working that night. It was obvious they knew each other.

After taking a few statements, Officer Eliot left the bar. She was only in there a few minutes, but the image of her in that uniform was forever ingrained in Talia's mind. She was incredibly hot, and Talia wanted badly to get up the courage to talk to her.

That night, Talia had wandered out to the parking lot to catch another glimpse. As she approached her squad car, Shay Eliot called back to the door where Dee stood. "Softball tomorrow?"

"Yep," the bartender had answered.

Talia had gone back into the bar then and asked one of the waitresses if she knew where she could watch some softball. She gave Talia the name of a park and directions.

Of course, Talia was there early the next morning, before anyone else. She walked around the park, until cars started to pull in. Then she got back in her car and waited until she saw Shay Eliot walking up to a ball field. Wearing jean shorts, a T-shirt with the sleeves rolled up, and a ball cap that allowed some light brown curls to peek out from the back, Talia thought she was even sexier than in her uniform. As she watched, Shay stopped suddenly and walked back in the direction she'd come. Talia was awestruck when Shay called out to see whose dog was in a nearby car. In a blur, she was breaking the window, getting a sluggish dog out, and yelling at a man who'd yelled at her about his car window.

"Do you know how hot it gets in a car? Are you clueless?" Shay asked.

When he threatened to call the police, she offered to do it for him. "Maybe they'll charge you with animal cruelty. Or maybe there will be multiple officers out on the road who know to watch you very carefully for every time you change lanes without a signal or go even one mile per hour over the speed limit. Yeah, let's do *that."* Talia never did learn what became of the poor dog, but she had a new hero.

Three months later, Talia was no closer to approaching Shay. By her third drink, she knew she wasn't going to be working up the nerve that night, and that angered her.

Just after eleven o'clock, when Shay started toward the door, Talia felt a boost of courage. She followed Shay out to the parking lot, meaning to catch up to Shay at their vehicles, but Shay was intercepted by a couple of women. Talia stayed back until they left.

Shay was pulling out of her parking spot as Talia approached. She jumped into her car and followed Shay out of the lot, trying to stay an inconspicuous distance from Shay's truck.

Talia stayed back while Shay pulled into her driveway, then parked and watched. The house was small, with a tidy yard. She could imagine Shay kneeling in the little flower garden, sweat causing her shirt to stick to her, her muscular arms glistening in the bright sunshine.

Around twelve thirty one of Shay's neighbors came out, walking a yellow Lab. They made a beeline for Shay's yard where the dog did its business and the woman ignored the concept of picking up after your dog. They walked down the road, returned ten minutes later, and then the woman came out with a golden retriever. This time the dog only urinated in Shay's yard. The third time the woman appeared she was walking a chow mix. This one crapped in Shay's yard then kicked its feet up several times, leaving ruts in Shay's otherwise perfectly manicured lawn.

Talia had to stop her legs from bouncing up and down. She was glad then that she'd only taken one robin egg. Any more than that and she would have been crawling out of her skin just sitting there.

She saw a flash of light and heard a "whoop" sound. She thought she was busted, then saw red and blue flashes of light between the houses, lighting up the night. It was a traffic stop going on one street over. *Please, God, don't let the police notice me over here.* She let out a huge breath when the cop and the other car left.

It started drizzling so she put the window up. She hated doing so, since it was a comfortable sixty degrees outside. Her windshield fogged up. Every time she wiped at the condensation she thought, *Wow, not very stealthy, Talia.*

†

Shay easily breezed through the three lawns she had scheduled for that Saturday. They were all in or near her neighborhood, so she didn't even have to drive anywhere, she just pushed the lawnmower from house to house with the edger thrown over her shoulder.

She thought again about the job Dee had offered her, working security at the bar. As the bar manager, Dee had been given full rein on hiring and firing, among other things. The idea of lurking in the parking lot as a rent-a-cop was not appealing, so Shay told her that she appreciated the offer, but would have to pass.

Once finished with the last yard of the day, she went home and hosed off the mower. After drinking several large glasses of water, she plopped down on the sofa with her phone. She was both looking forward to and dreading this phone call. *Just call*, she told herself. She dialed the number.

"Hi, Mom."

"What's wrong?" Cynthia Eliot asked.

"What do you mean, 'what's wrong?' I'm just calling to say hello. I call. It's not like I never call," Shay said, feeling defensive.

"I know you call. But when you start out with 'Hi, Mom,' something is wrong. When you start out with 'Hey, there!' I know all is well. A mother knows these things. A mother learns these details."

"Are you finished?" Shay teased.

"Yes. No. Now tell me what's wrong," Cynthia said.

"I quit the police force."

"Oh, thank God!"

Shay almost choked.

"I hated you working that job. It's dangerous. Not to mention you meet all the wrong kinds of women doing that work."

Shay put her feet up on the coffee table. She knew she might be there a while.

"So," Cynthia said, "what are you going to do now?"

Shay pictured her, hands on hips, gray hair hanging stylishly to her chin. Her mother had turned completely gray by the time she reached forty. Shay figured she shared that gene, considering that since turning twenty-nine several months earlier she'd been noticing more gray mixing in with her brown. "I guess I'll mow lawns until I figure something else out."

"You need money? I could send you some money."

Shay could visualize her mom going through her purse, pulling a stashed twenty- or fifty-dollar bill from this or that pocket, starting a small pile of miscellaneous bills in the middle of the kitchen table. "No Mom, I don't need any money."

"You can come back to Richmond now that there's nothing stopping you from coming home. You are a bright woman and could easily pick things up at your father's office."

"I can't see myself working in Real Estate. Besides, Norfolk is home now. I have my house here. And my friends."

"There are lesbians in Richmond, you know." Cynthia made a sound that resembled a stifled chuckle. "They have their own bars and bookstores here too, you know."

"I know, Mom." She flashed in her mind to when she'd come out to her parents. Her mom was only worried for her 'little girl's' happiness. Her dad said nothing. Shay still wasn't sure if he'd heard the proclamation since his hearing was suspect even then, years earlier.

"Do you have a girlfriend yet?"

Shay had made the mistake of confiding in her mom once about how, as long as she was a cop, she didn't know if she wanted to get into a relationship. She didn't want to put anyone through all the funky hours or the worrying about her.

"Now you have no excuse," Cynthia said. "Get yourself a sweetheart. Coupled people live longer— it's a proven fact."

"I will make finding a girlfriend my number two priority. I promise." Poke jumped up on her lap and she petted him.

"Second? Why second?"

"Because my first priority has to be to find satisfying work."

"With that attitude, you'll never meet the right girl."

Shay decided to leave that one alone. She wasn't about to tell her mom that the only person she'd even thought about being with for years was already in a relationship, and that she considered both her and her girlfriend to be good friends. "Enough about my boring life. Tell me what you and Dad have been up to."

"Well, your father is still deaf as a doorknob. He refuses to get a hearing aid because he says it'll make him look like an old man. So I tell him, 'You *are* an old man.'"

Shay mouthed along with the last words, knowing them well.

Her mom continued. "As if holding his hand up to his ear and saying, 'Eh? Eh?' doesn't make him look old."

Shay smiled at the image that conjured. She spent a few more minutes assuring her mom that she didn't need any money but would let her know if she did, then she got off the phone. She felt better after talking to her mom, and wasn't sure why she doubted she would.

She decided she should work on a project. She gave Poke one last rub behind the ears and slid out from under his skinny body.

Shay went into her one-car garage and eyed the cans of paint stacked in the corner of the small space. The area wasn't big enough to comfortably park her pickup, but it worked well for her tools and some of the yard equipment. She'd bought the paint months ago, back when she was more gainfully employed. She had more money than time then. That was no longer the case.

She took the tape and tarps off the shelf, then gathered the other painting supplies and carried them into the house. She lugged in a can of paint, then hauled in the ladder. Once the ladder was out of the way, she eyed the punching bag in the corner of the garage. Not today, but soon, she told herself. Soon she would get back to what she liked to call her 'fighting shape.'

Four hours later, she surveyed her work. She allowed herself a beer once she'd finished painting all the ceilings. Her legs were sore from going up and down the ladder. Her neck hurt from the awkward position she'd been in for far too long. It all made her feel surprisingly good.

She removed the tape protecting the walls but left the tarps down. Poke had managed to get under the tarp on the sofa and kept screaming like it was killing him, but every time Shay would go to his rescue, he'd act unimpressed and return to the excitement under the tarp.

After a few more Amstel Lights, Shay knew she wasn't going anywhere. Besides, it probably wouldn't be healthy for her to go out every night. Not to mention the financial strain of doing so.

†

It was Saturday night and Talia drove slowly past the parking lot of the bar, looking for Shay's pickup. An array of vehicles— from sedans and station wagons to pickup trucks and Jeeps—filled the parking lot. When she was sure Shay's truck wasn't tucked up by the building or hidden near the bank, she headed toward Shay's house.

Talia took the same route as the night before, and then pulled to the side of the road three houses away. It was far enough not to be too obvious, but not so far that she wouldn't see if Shay came out. Shay's truck was parked in the driveway, the same crooked position it was in the night before. Talia wondered if Shay had stayed in all day, and if so, what she had been doing.

It was another drizzly night, another night of fogging the windows of her car. She loved her Honda. Brian had been so proud of the silver sedan when he'd brought it home. He said it reeked of class. When he knew he was going down for embezzling, he sold the car to Talia drastically cheap. He made her swear to him that she would take really good care of it. He didn't expect it back when he got out, but he did expect to see it in good shape. She didn't want to disappoint him.

As she sat watching for Shay, she started to fabricate stories as to why she was sitting a few doors down from Shay Eliot's house. Once she came up with one, she would have to memorize it. Rehearse it. Because if ever called out, if ever forced to give her story to someone, she'd have to stick to it. That was the biggest lesson she'd learned from her older brother: once you put something to words, you never changed them. No matter what pressure was put on you, you never caved.

Talia's heart raced at the memory of her first lesson on not changing course once you've said something. She was ten years old and had lied to Timmy Hall about riding his bike without his permission. At first she'd held her own against his accusation. But then his brother Tommy said he'd seen her on Timmy's bike. Faced with an eyewitness, Talia admitted she had. Timmy pushed her. She'd seen her brother watching then. Four years older than Talia, Brian was always her ally against their parents and the authorities at school so she was sure he'd come to her aid. But he hadn't. He'd stood there, leaning against a tree, and allowed Timmy Hall to shove her around for a good five minutes. It wasn't until Timmy said, "And piss on you," and started to undo his pants that Brian had finally said, "Enough." Talia cried as she followed her brother home. On their front steps he said to her, "If you don't stick to your story, you pay the price. Don't ever let me see you back down on your story again."

And she hadn't. Which was why she was so shocked when Brian had gone against his own advice, and now was serving a seven-year prison term.

Talia's attempt at coming up with a story was interrupted when a truck with the Calz's Pizza and Wings logo painted on its side pulled up in front of Shay's house around ten thirty. Talia watched as the driver knocked on the wooden front door, and Shay answered almost immediately. She traded money for the pizza and disappeared back inside.

†

At least once a month, usually on Sundays, Shay got together for dinner with Kate and Lana. She glanced around the table, glad to be at dinner with such good friends. It was not lost on Shay that they always invited a friend along to these dinners, their attempt to fix Shay up, she was sure. She stole a glance across the table at Jennifer, tonight's offering. She was very nice, and quite attractive, but Shay wasn't interested.

They were at her favorite restaurant, Chi-Chi's. The waiter handed out menus and asked whether or not it would all be on one check. Shay quickly spoke up, "You can put me on my own." She wanted to set the tone that this was not a double date before things went any further.

Once everyone was sipping their margaritas, the waiter returned for their food orders. They had to stop midway through while the rest of the staff sang happy birthday to a woman wearing a huge sombrero. Jennifer sang along and clapped when it was over. Shay added a little clap of her own. Why not? They were out to have a good time and Shay intended to do just that.

When the food was served, Shay smiled down at the plate of seafood nachos. For now, she could still afford their dinners out. If she didn't figure out soon what she wanted to be when she grew up, she would be eating PB&J for lunch every day and macaroni and cheese for most dinners. She picked up a chip smothered in seafood and cheese and took a bite. All her cares disappeared.

Shay looked up when she heard Kate laughing.

"What?" Shay asked.

"You were totally blissing out on that nacho," Kate said.

"Good food is something to savor."

"Like good friendships," Jennifer said, raising her margarita glass.

"Like good friendships," the other three echoed. They all clanked glasses.

Their attention was drawn to where voices were raised on the other side of the restaurant. Shay and Lana exchanged glances when they realized one of those voices belonged to Paulie.

"Quit staring at me, you fruit!"

"Oh, you know you're flattered. If your *girlfriend* wasn't with you, you'd be all into me and you know it," Paulie said.

The man turned three shades of red and Shay wondered if Paulie was on to something. But it didn't matter if he was. Paulie was being rude. Apparently his dinner companion thought so too because he kept trying to shush Paulie.

"And he wonders why he gets beat up all the time," Jennifer mumbled.

Shay didn't even know how to respond. Except for self-defense or the defense of others, there was no excuse for violence. Ever. And the violence against Paulie, even if not the reason for her lack of a career in law enforcement, had been a catalyst for it. She opened her mouth to say something, saw the pained look on Kate's face, and decided against it.

Her attention was drawn back to Paulie's table. It appeared the manager was asking him to please keep it down. Paulie's voice got louder and louder. He accused the manager of being a homophobe as he made a big scene of getting up and marching toward the exit. He stopped just as he was passing their table.

"Look, the girls are out," he said to no one since his dinner companion was still at their table, paying the bill and apologizing to everyone around them. "Oh, and it's the po-lice," he said as he gestured toward Shay. "I would like you to arrest that man over there." He pointed to the guy he'd had the original altercation with. "Arrest him for being in the closet."

"Ignore him," Shay muttered.

When he saw he wasn't going to get a rise out of her, he sauntered away.

"Isn't he suing the city for police brutality?" Jennifer asked.

"Yep," Lana answered through clenched teeth. She and Shay had had a long conversation when that news came out. Lana had voiced her opinion that suing was Paulie's main motivation all along, and Shay's job was collateral damage.

"Enough about him," Kate announced. "Jennifer, how is it going with the power company?"

Jennifer talked about her job a little, then asked Lana about bartending, and asked Shay why she wasn't a cop anymore.

Shay glanced toward the table where Paulie had been.

"Oh, tired of dealing with trash like him, huh?"

"Something like that," Shay said.

The rest of dinner had gone well. Shay was confident, between the separate check and not lingering while saying goodnight to Jennifer, that she'd gotten it across she wasn't interested in dating her or anyone else Kate and Lana tried to fix her up with. She was comfortable sitting back and waiting. She didn't want to date for the sake of dating; she wanted to wait for the one person who really grabbed her attention and didn't let go.

Back at home, Shay changed into sweats and went into the garage to hit on the punching bag. The last thing she wanted to do was get out of shape.

✝

Talia drove down the Colonial Parkway in Yorktown, looking for Fish, who she'd heard, finally, had some decent pot. She'd left the bar early Sunday evening because Shay wasn't there, driven by Shay's house, like she had the night before, but Shay's truck wasn't there so Talia left. She'd returned once more to the bar, just in case Shay turned up late, but hadn't stayed too long. Now, Talia's mind drifted, wondering where Shay was and who she was with. Talia knew her infatuation for Shay was bordering on pathetic, but couldn't seem to help herself.

Part of Talia was still shaken up over being chased the other night, but another part refused to let it alter her routine too much. She had her window down, enjoying the cool mid-fifties temperature, but also knew if she saw a dark-colored van she would roll up the window as fast as possible and floor it out of there.

She loved the parkway. She loved the scenery and the way you didn't see billboards or restaurants, or any other businesses along the way. She loved how her car tires sounded on the rounded river gravel that was set in concrete, the look of the brick of the overpasses, the rich, centuries-long history of the road and surrounding areas. She felt lucky to have grown up in such a cool place.

It was Columbus Day. Or had been. Now it was nearly two in the morning of the Tuesday after. Luckily Talia was off through Wednesday because Dr. Bennett had gone away for a very long weekend, and when he took off, the entire office also had to.

She sang along to Sam Harris as he belted out "Over the Rainbow." She loved his first album and had already worn out one other copy of the cassette. In between songs, a yawn snuck up on

26

her. She was about to turn around and head home when she saw the flash of police lights.

A parade of law enforcement vehicles filled a pull-off. There were York County deputies, Park Service rangers, and state troopers—some had their lights on, strobes of color lighting up the trees, and some didn't. Parked to the side was a black van. The hair on the back of Talia's neck stood on end. Was that *the* van? Or was the van that had chased her dark blue? Her stomach twisted.

She turned off the music and drove by at a crawl. She could hear a cacophony of broken radio chatter from the different law enforcement officers. She noticed the back end of a car protruding from the heavy brush to the right of the pull-off. A park ranger walked in her direction. He was big and scary and when he motioned for her to move on, she did. She glanced back at the black van one last time and saw a white bundle being loaded into it. She had always thought that body bags were black. She shivered—and got the hell out of there.

Chapter Three

Talia walked into the bar and was struck by how off it felt. There was no music, no clinking and clanking from the pool tables, and everyone spoke in hushed tones. Talia didn't think about her shyness and insecurities when she sat two stools down from Shay.

"Can I get you a drink?" the bartender, Dee, asked.

She ordered a vodka and tonic. Once Dee had placed her change on the bar in front of her, Dee's attention went back to Shay. Talia turned slightly to listen in on their conversation.

"The newspapers called them friends," Dee said to Shay.

Talia thought about the article detailing the grisly death of two women on the parkway. She'd read it so many times she'd almost memorized it. And all around York County no one spoke about anything but the murders. It was a big deal. Nothing like that had ever happened here before.

"*Friends*," Dee repeated.

"Of course they did."

"Are they clueless?"

Shay shrugged. "Or maybe they wanted to make it more palatable for the public so they'd give a shit."

"It just feels so...so..."

"Dismissive?" Shay asked.

"Yes. That. Exactly."

"Yeah," Shay whispered. She took a sip of her drink.

Talia thought Shay looked tired.

"What have you heard about it?" Dee asked.

"What do you mean?" Shay asked.

"What are your cop buddies saying?"

"They aren't saying anything to me." Shay turned Talia's way but seemed to look right through her. Talia's feelings would have been hurt if the expression on Shay's face hadn't been one of such utter defeat.

Talia's attention was drawn to the far corner of the bar where a group of four women were huddled, sobbing in each other's arms. She knew instinctively that they were friends of the murdered women. Talia pushed her drink aside. She couldn't take it. As much as she wanted to numb herself, she didn't think she could keep it down.

The image of the mystery van's headlights flashing in the rearview mirror...the pungent scent of pot lingering in her car...the flashing lights of the police cars...the stark finality of a white body bag being loaded into the back of a black van...the sound of broken radio chatter mixing with the pounding of her heart...the way the images of two different nights mixed in Talia's head and gut transfixed her in the middle of this horrific, sad, and maddening tragedy. But sitting on the stool at the bar she wasn't in the middle of anything. She was once again on the outside. She didn't think she knew either of the women, and wouldn't lie, wouldn't embellish, wouldn't dirty this moment with a sick need to claim some attention for herself.

When Talia looked back, Dee gave her a sad, connecting wink after noticing her largely untouched drink. Kate nodded at Talia when their eyes met, a movement that included Talia in this place with this pain. Yes, everyone in the bar hurt. Everyone felt the pain of having members of their community savagely ripped away. Whether they knew them personally or not, someone had murdered two of their own.

The lack of music finally sank in. Talia realized the DJ was in the huddle of crying women. The quiet must have registered with others then because there were murmurs of turning on some tunes. "And please," she heard someone say, "don't let it be sad."

Shay got off her barstool and walked over to the DJ. She whispered something in her ear and the DJ nodded. Shay went into the DJ booth and fiddled around a bit.

"Does she know what she's doing?" Kate asked.

"She dated a DJ once. Just long enough to learn her way around the booth," Dee said.

Several women laughed. Talia wasn't amused. She hated the prospect of Shay dating anyone who wasn't her.

Madonna's voice came out of the speakers.

There was a collective sigh of relief. Talia wondered if the others expected to hear Patsy Cline.

†

The next night Talia thought about staying at home, but she couldn't make herself stay away from the bar. Something had happened that would change every one of their lives in some way and she wouldn't, couldn't look away from it.

She sat down on the stool next to Shay. Talia didn't look at her as she asked in a low voice, "Did you know them?"

Shay stared forward. "I knew Allie," she said.

"I'm sorry." Talia turned to her.

Shay turned to look at her and her steel-blue eyes almost stole the breath right out of Talia. "Did you know them?"

Words raced through her head. *Do not lie. Do not lie. Do not be a Liarhead Lizard.* The memory of her and Brian getting caught in a lie by his girlfriend, Nancy, came into Talia's head in mega-color and full-stereo sound. Nancy was screaming, "Liar! Liarhead! You're Liarhead Lishers!" Her words had started roaring out of her faster and faster until they morphed into Liarhead Lizards. It took no time at all for the moniker to make it to school—it ended up whispered, muttered, shouted through the hallways, scribbled on their lockers—and it was totally believable because the Lisher family had indeed gotten quite the reputation for making things up.

Talia shook her head. "No, I don't think I knew them." Relief washed over her. She'd gotten the words out without lying, without embellishing. Her relief, though, was immediately eclipsed by the enormity of the situation, the heinous brutality of it.

They sat in silence. Talia was trying to form words to continue the conversation when they were interrupted. A woman she'd seen around the bar sat on the other side of Shay. Holding her beer bottle with a white-knuckled grip, she turned to Shay and said, "Why aren't they going after that bastard ex-husband? You know that redneck either did it himself or had them killed. We all know they were slaughtered because he couldn't deal with being dumped for a dyke. But no"—her voice rose higher— "no, instead they go after the ex-girlfriend because of course the lesbo is the killer, right? This is bullshit. Regina introduced them, for crying out loud. She wanted them to be happy together. The fucking FBI needs to leave her alone and go after the redneck!"

Talia stared at the bar, afraid to make eye contact with the woman who was so full of anger.

"That's enough," Shay said. Then she was interrupted by someone else who'd leaned between them.

"It was a cop," the new woman said. "It looked just like a traffic stop. Besides, the husband has an iron-clad alibi. And we all know it wasn't anyone who knew Allie and Diane. Everyone who knew them loved them. It had to be random. Or because they were lesbians."

"Of course it was because they were lesbians," Dee chimed in.

For so long Talia had wanted to be at the center of things at the bar, especially with Shay, but she was feeling overwhelmed. Everyone was too close, too loud, too angry. Talia grew dizzy.

Talia turned to Shay and felt immediate relief when their eyes met.

"Excuse us," Shay said to no one and everyone. "Coming?" she asked Talia.

Talia nodded, and they squeezed their way out of the small group of women who had formed around them. The mix of voices continued as they walked away. "It was the fucking redneck!"

"No, it was a park ranger!"

"Or the CIA!"

"You okay?" Shay asked as they increased the distance from the others. "You look a little pale."

"It was all just too much," Talia said.

"Yeah, I know." Shay squeezed her shoulder and smiled. "I have to get out of here. Don't let those women get to you, okay?"

Talia nodded, then watched as Shay walked out of the bar.

Talia thought about going after her, but Lana followed Shay out. Talia knew she couldn't compete with Lana for Shay's attention, just like she knew she couldn't compete with Kate for Shay's attention either.

†

Shay squatted by the flower garden in her backyard, pulling a weed here and there, but her heart wasn't in it. She wandered around the yard, knowing there was plenty of work she could do, but unable to commit to any one task.

She'd been thinking about the murders. She didn't know much about Diane, just that Allie was the first woman she'd been with. Every time Shay asked Allie when she would get to meet her new girlfriend, Allie would promise her soon. She'd said that Diane was nervous about anyone knowing about their relationship.

Shay had been thrilled for Allie. She was happier than Shay had seen her in a long time. Things were looking good, not just in her new relationship, but also in her job. Allie had gotten a promotion at the financial services company she'd been working for ever since graduating from Old Dominion University three years earlier.

Shay plopped down on the grass that was in need of a good mowing. She plucked at a few straggly blades as tears coursed down her face. She couldn't believe what had happened to Allie and Diane. She couldn't make sense of it.

She sprawled on her back and let the sun burn her eyes. Just as she was about to shut them, she saw movement in her peripheral vision. She rolled onto her side and let Poke do a kitty head-butt against her forehead. She pulled him to her and he didn't resist as she snuggled against him, letting her tears come freely against his skinny side.

Shay thought about Allie at their softball games. She packed a lot of power into her five-foot-three frame. She could hit to any field and nothing got past her at third. She was so fair-skinned that she reapplied sunscreen after every inning or two. And the more she was in the sun, the lighter and lighter her hair got until it was almost white by the end of each summer.

She drifted off. Sometime later, Poke got restless so Shay let him up. The sun had sunk low in the sky and Shay felt a slight coolness in the air. She got up and followed Poke to the back door. She knew he'd be looking for food. And she wanted a drink.

She put kibble in Poke's bowl and added a spoon of canned tuna. She opened the fridge to grab a beer but just couldn't do it. If she drank alone she would cry all night long. She didn't think her eyes could handle any more tears, so she grabbed her car keys and headed out.

Shay was at the bar in only a few minutes. She plopped down on a barstool and hoped she looked better than she felt after her crying jag. "Amstel Light," she told Dee.

After setting the beer on the bar, Dee nodded to the right. "Your fan club is here again." Shay looked over by the jukebox and caught the young woman with the big hair and purple eye shadow watching her. Well, she assumed the eye shadow was purple since that's what it usually was. The young woman looked away quickly.

Dee had teased Shay before about the 'strays' she tended to attract. After spending a few moments with the young woman right after the murders, Shay now thought of her as a little lost, but not a stray. She was always uncomfortable when Dee talked about people like that.

She thought about going over to where the young woman leaned against the jukebox, but before she could another equally young woman dragged her out onto the dance floor. Shay watched them dance. It was probably for the best. Shay didn't want to encourage her since she was way too young.

Shay stared at the mirrored wall and focused on two palm prints. They were in locations that told her someone had most likely stood with a hand on each side of a lover's head, maybe even leaned in for a kiss. She mentally went through the motion of lifting the prints from the mirror. She hated that the image had immediately shifted in her head to resemble a crime scene needing evidence collection so she quickly turned away.

"Considering all that has happened," Shay said to Dee, "maybe I will do some parking lot security for the bar. If the offer is still there."

Dee smiled. "Of course the offer is still there. The pay isn't great, but it is something. And I know every woman in here will feel better knowing you're out there."

✝

Over the next couple of weeks Talia heard a lot of conflicting information, mostly a blur of conspiracy theories. One rumor was the ex-husband's family owned the auto shop that worked on all the area law enforcement vehicles, and the cops weren't looking close enough at the man because of those ties. Another story was that a rogue CIA agent was out hunting people and that there had been others, but they had been covered up. The one thing that was consistent, though, was the anxiety over how Allie's ex-girlfriend was being mistreated by the investigators.

And there was plenty of anxiety—over the deaths of the women, the investigation, and the absence of answers.

Halloween came and Talia looked forward to the distraction of a good party. And, she'd heard the bar always threw a great one. What to be, what to be? was the question that provided some relief from the constant buzz about the murders.

When she finally decided to go as a mummy, she drove to the drugstore to buy some gauze wrap. As a five-foot-five cashier dressed as Bat-girl rang up her purchase at the register, she felt like she was being watched. She looked up to see April Hunter, Kate's younger sister. Talia nodded an acknowledgment and was surprised when April walked out with her.

"Hi," Talia said.

"Hey. I wasn't sure if you were still in the area. How've you been?"

"Good," Talia said, looking her over. April had gained quite a bit of weight, which wasn't necessarily a bad thing, considering how thin she was the last few times Talia had seen her. "What have you been up to?"

"You know, same old," April mumbled. She looked around and leaned a little closer. "Do you by chance have anything for—for ah, energy?"

"I don't have much but I could spot you a few black beauties."

"I don't need much," she said as she seemed to brighten. "I don't really use the stuff anymore but I just need a little something."

Talia remembered then that she didn't have any with her, it was all at home. And since she was also trying to impress a certain ex-cop, who was good friends with April's sister, did she really want to be the one who gave April some illegal drugs? And if April was trying to get her life together, did she want to be the one who screwed that up?

"Oh, wow," Talia said, patting her pockets. "You know, I just remembered I took the last bit yesterday. I'm sorry."

It was hard to watch April almost crumble under her news, but Talia wasn't risking anything about drugs getting back to Shay. She thought then how she was going to quit with the beauties and hearts and robin eggs, and stick to the legal caffeine of Jolt Cola. She apologized again to April, then got in her car and left the drugstore parking lot.

†

Knowing she would need some help with her costume, Talia had enlisted the assistance of her fellow dental office peon, Lacey. They were going in opposite directions for their parties—Talia to Norfolk and Lacey to Richmond—so they met at Talia's apartment. She helped Lacey with her white face paint for her vampire costume and Lacey wrapped Talia. They were running behind because they'd taken a break or two to hit the pipe and weed Lacey had brought over with her.

As they ran out the door to their cars, Talia's neighbor was walking up the steps to her apartment and stopped short. "Hi, Talia. Wow. Look at you two."

Lacey bared her fangs and hissed. Talia lifted her arm in a stiff half wave. Talia was hoping she wouldn't have to introduce Lacey because she only knew her neighbor as the Maybe Lesbian from across the way. Since the woman knew her name, Talia assumed they'd introduced themselves at some point when Talia was either too drunk or too stoned to remember. Now she was too embarrassed to admit she didn't remember it or to take the time to ask.

"I forgot it was Halloween. I guess I better run out and get some candy," Maybe Lesbian said before pivoting around and starting back down the stairs.

Talia knew she should eventually learn the woman's name. She kept expecting to run into her at the bar but never did. She was attractive, but not Talia's type, and, well, she was no Shay Eliot. She gave another half wave before turning her attention to her car.

As Talia carefully folded herself into the front seat of her car, she realized driving was going to be an issue. Vampire Lacey laughed at her. "I guess you better pick a lane and not leave it until you get there. Good luck!"

Talia had to turn her whole body to look in either direction. Her biggest fear was that she'd pull her mummy wrappings loose and not know how to put it back together. Lacey had done a great job wrapping her, but Talia was starting to have second thoughts about her costume's restrictions.

Talia relaxed a little when she made it to the interstate. She glanced to her left and smiled at the tree in the middle of the median. As was customary, the old Christmas tree that had been mysteriously planted in the median was decorated for Halloween. She could see the orange of pumpkins and the white of ghosts, but not much else. She made a mental note to look closer the next time she passed during the day.

Traffic slowed at the tunnel, of course, and as Talia was crawling along she felt someone staring at her. She pivoted her body around and caught a peek at a clown as it blew her a kiss. She would have blown one back but clowns freaked her out and the traffic had picked up the pace so she turned her body and head forward.

Once in Norfolk, she went through intersections holding her breath, praying for safety because that was easier than trying to look both ways. Relief washed over her as she pulled into the parking lot at the bar, until she realized she had to pee and would have to partially unwrap to do so. What in the hell was she thinking dressing as a mummy?

The image of angry witches, vamps, and maybe even killer clowns waiting in line for her to unwrap, pee, and rewrap in the ladies' room terrorized her. The parking lot was already crowded so she knew the party was well underway. Shay's truck was there so Talia assumed she was inside the bar.

Talia got out of the car and decided she'd sneak between the two buildings and pee there before going in. On the way to her chosen spot, she started a mantra in her head. *Stay inside Shay, stay inside.* She wondered if Shay would be dressed in costume now that she was doing security for the bar. She couldn't wait to see. But first, she had to attend to the business of her ready-to-burst bladder.

Walking with the stiff-legged gait of a mummy, Talia turned her whole body at the sound of people approaching. Two women, one wearing a blond wig, both with throats slashed and bloodied clothing came toward her. It took a moment to sink in. Bile rose in her throat and pee soiled her wrappings. The women laughed and walked toward the bar.

Talia half-ran and half-tripped to her car. She rummaged in the backseat for a plastic bag to sit on. She was shaking as she started ripping the gauze wrapping from around her head and neck. Breathing was difficult. Finally free of the gauze, she rolled down the window for some air, then started her car. Hearing a commotion, she paused before pulling out.

Dee stood in the doorway, yelling at the two women. "What were you thinking? Get the hell out of here!"

Then Shay was there, dressed as a gangster. Talia was mortified at the thought of being seen in a pee-soiled costume. She dropped the car in gear and hightailed it out of the parking lot.

At least Talia wasn't the only one with a strong reaction to seeing the women. But she was sure she was the only one they made pee on themselves. She felt tears on her cheeks as she drove away. *So much for a good distraction.*

Chapter Four

Shay sat down at the table across from FBI Agent Timothy Grainger. She wasn't surprised when she was asked to come in to answer a few questions. She'd heard enough chatter around the bar to know they were looking at anyone who dealt with diesel fuel, and that they were particularly interested in anyone who was ex-law enforcement.

Grainger offered her coffee or a soda. She declined. She looked at the tan-painted cinder block walls until the agent spoke.

"How well did you know Allison Bradford and Diane Fields?"

"I knew Allie quite well, but I haven't met—hadn't—met Diane yet."

"How did you meet Allison?"

Shay fought against the tears that threatened. Just keep it together, she told herself. "The first time I saw her was years ago at a softball game. We were on opposite teams and her team won. She came up to me afterward and said she liked my game." Shay laughed, lost in the memory. She was pretty sure at the time that Allie had come up to her mostly to get a chance to talk to Anne, whom she had ended up dating for a while afterward. "Allie was very competitive and a damned good ball player."

"Who out there didn't like Allison as much as you seem to?"

"Everyone who knew Allie loved Allie. She was that great of a person."

Agent Grainger slid a piece of paper across the table to Shay. "Write down the name of every woman you know who has dated Allison. First and last names, please."

Shay stared at the blank paper. If she thought for even a minute that this would get them closer to finding Allie and Diane's murderer, she'd be writing like mad. But this felt a lot like a witch hunt and she couldn't see herself playing a role in that.

"No one who knew her could have killed her. And especially no one who dated her could ever hurt her. You are looking in the wrong direction, sir."

He slammed his fist down on the table. "Don't tell me how to investigate a murder. You couldn't cut it as a patrol officer and you're going to second-guess how I perform a murder investigation?"

"I know you know how to conduct a murder investigation, but what you don't know is how the dynamics of the lesbian community work. You won't get anywhere if this is how you're treating every woman you have come in here for an interview." Shay hated that her voice shook but she was too angry to be able to stop it.

"When's the last time you saw Allison?" He seemed to have regained his composure.

Images flashed through her mind—the cookout, one night at the bar, a softball game. "About a month and a half ago. No, maybe it was two months."

"Was she with someone?"

"I think the last time I saw her we were at a cookout. There were a lot of people there but she wasn't there with anyone in particular."

"Were the two of you ever involved?"

"No."

"Did you want to be?"

"No."

"Why not?"

"What do you mean, why not? Not every lesbian wants to be with every other lesbian."

"But you've been in here talking like she was *it*. Why wouldn't you want to be with her if she was so terrific?"

Shay could feel the muscles in her jaw tightening.

"When's the last time *you* were with someone?" he asked.

Shay leaned forward slightly. "That's none of your business."

"Oh, but it is. Every little thing about you is my business." He stared at her. "Someone reported you for damage to personal property while you were a police officer. What can you tell me about that?"

Shay racked her brain, trying to pinpoint the episode.

"You don't remember?"

She shrugged.

"You don't remember breaking a man's window because his dog was inside the car?"

Oh, yeah, that. "Yes, I remember that. I remember it was very hot and the dog could have died in that car."

"You like taking the law into your own hands?"

"Not particularly."

"You think you're above the law?"

"Not particularly."

"What, only when someone deserves it?"

Shay didn't respond. She knew he was trying to provoke her and she wasn't planning to give him the satisfaction.

"Or just when you want justice? Who did you want justice for this time, huh? Did you get justice for Allie's ex, huh? Did you get justice for Regina Morris?" he asked in rapid-fire mode.

She stared at the wall over his left shoulder, tuning him out as she refused to hear another word. He responded by shoving some photos across the table in front of her. The force of the pictures being pushed at her made her look down, and she jumped slightly when she realized what they were.

"Pretty graphic, aren't they?" he said.

Shay looked up at him.

"Don't look away from those pictures!" He practically came across the table trying to push them closer to her. "Allie's throat is cut so deep she was almost decapitated. That takes a lot of rage. That takes a lot of *personal* rage."

She fought against the taste of bile. She had seen many graphic crime scenes and crime scene pictures, but never of anyone that she knew well.

"Her tongue was severed," he said. "That's a lot of anger."

She glanced down again. She didn't want to see the images, not really, but thought if she looked closer she might see something that could make sense of the senselessness. She was pretty sure she'd never have access to the photos again and wanted to get the best possible observation. She picked up the picture that best showed the positions of both women inside Diane's Honda.

"Reliving the moment?" he asked.

She looked over all the photos as fast as she could. She cringed at the way Diane was shoved into the backseat and the way Allie was half on the seat and half on the passenger side floor, her light hair matted in several directions. The glove box door had been ripped off and its contents dumped on top of her.

Grainger's voice penetrated again. "Did you strike those matches over and over and over trying to hide what you'd done?"

That's when she noticed Allie and Diane had been doused in something and there were dozens of matches scattered about.

"How did you get them to go along? Did you surprise them with your badge and by the time Allison realized it was you it was too late for her to respond?"

"Enough. I've heard enough of this nonsense," Shay said.

"You don't want to hear about how you tried to push Diane's car into the river to hide how you'd slit their throats and tried to burn their bodies?" His face was bright red and spittle flew as he yelled.

"Either arrest me or I'm leaving. Either way, don't come near me without my lawyer present." Her throat tasted like acid, and she wondered how in the hell she would afford a lawyer.

"Get the hell out of here. For now." He picked up a close-up of Allie's wounds and pushed it into Shay's face. "I will prove that you did this. You wait and see."

Shay kept her gait steady as she walked to her car. It took a lot of effort not to run, but she would not give him the satisfaction of seeing how badly he'd upset her. Halfway home, she pulled over to the side of the road and threw up. With every heave she closed her eyes but forced them open to keep from revisiting the bloody mess in the pictures. She pulled over twice more to throw up before she made it home.

That night, every time she closed her eyes, she saw Allie's and Diane's faces. Her phone rang several times, but she couldn't make herself answer.

When she tried to sleep, the images assaulted her. She dreamed about coming across the car on the parkway and shining a flashlight inside, seeing the bloodied faces. But the faces in her dream were Kate's and Lana's. After she awoke and finally quit shaking, she wondered what that meant. She knew she could never ask her favorite shrink-to-be, Kate. No, she would never tell anyone about the twist to her nightmare.

The next morning, the phone rang relentlessly. Shay lay in bed and let it ring. She knew she had to get up and get ready to mow some yards, but she felt sick and tired and couldn't stop crying.

The doorbell made her jump. Stumbling out of bed and to the door she looked out the peephole and saw Kate standing there.

"I know you're in there," Kate said. "Please let me in."

Shay opened the door and stepped to the side. Before she shut the door, she looked outside to see if any law enforcement were watching her house. There was a questionable black sedan parked three doors down.

"You want to tell me about yesterday?" Kate asked as she stepped into the middle of the living room.

"Not really. How do you know about yesterday?"

"Dee told me."

Shay's eyes narrowed.

"Don't be upset with her. She's worried about you. She said she's had a bad feeling ever since the FBI came into the bar asking about you."

"Want something to drink?" Shay asked.

"No. I can't stay too long. I have class soon but I wanted to see you. To know you're okay."

"I'm okay."

"You don't look okay."

Shay shrugged.

"You don't always have to be the strong one. You can talk to me, you know."

"I know." But she didn't. "I'm sorry. I can't talk about this right now."

"When you are ready, let me know. I'm a good listener, and you've listened to my problems enough over the years. Let me be here for you for once. Okay?"

"Okay."

"Are you working today?"

"Yeah. As soon as I eat something."

"Call me if you need me." Kate said as she left.

Shay shut the door behind Kate and locked it. She pressed her forehead against the door and closed her eyes. Then she opened them, trying to make the images of Allie and Diane get out of her head.

The tears began again.

✝

Talia knew not much happened in their community that did not end up being whispered, fought over, or cried about in the bar. So when Talia overheard Dee grilling Lana and Kate about Shay's interview with the FBI, Talia's focus became laser-sharp to hear what they were saying.

It seemed that because Shay knew Allie, was ex-law enforcement, and currently had access to diesel fuel through her landscaping business, the FBI was looking at her closely.

The newspapers were still running stories about how it looked like the assailant was either a cop, or pretended to be one, because the scene looked like a traffic stop. Diane's wallet was opened to her driver's license on the center console, as if she'd been showing her ID.

Talia tried not to think about what diesel fuel had to do with anything, but couldn't help forming an image. It made her feel nauseated.

"Oh, God, poor Eliot," Kate said.

Talia moved closer and leaned against the bar, as if she was watching the action at the pool tables opposite them.

"She has an alibi. She was here," Lana said.

"Not every night in question," Dee corrected her. "They are looking at Thursday through Sunday nights."

"Because Allie and Diane were last seen at Cinema City on Thursday?" Kate asked.

"Yeah, and not found until Monday. No one saw Shay late on Friday night or at all on Saturday night."

Talia swung around on her barstool so fast that she clanked loudly against the stool next to hers. Dee, Lana, and Kate all looked at her. She opened her mouth to speak, but no words came out. Instead, she got up and went into the ladies' room. She was going to splash water on her face but the sight of mascara smudged under her eyes stopped her. She spent several minutes cleaning up the mess and adjusting her hair. When another woman came in, Talia quickly excused herself and left the claustrophobic space.

It wasn't difficult to find a business card with an FBI agent's name and number on it. No one wanted to talk to them so they'd left cards behind as a reminder that they were looking for information. The cards had been littering the bar for weeks. Talia snatched one off the top of the cigarette machine and shoved it into her pocket for later.

†

Talia waited until after work the next day to call the FBI. Her hands shook as she held the phone in one and the card in the other. She was terrified, but there was no way she was going to let them harass Shay Eliot when she knew exactly where she was on the nights in question.

Talia leaned against the kitchen wall as she dialed the number. She asked to speak to the Agent Jackson listed on the card and waited patiently for him to come to the phone. She was about to hang up when a deep voice broke through the silence and introduced himself as Agent Jackson.

At first she stammered, then she managed to say, "I know where Shay Eliot was on Friday and Saturday night before those women were found murdered on the Colonial Parkway."

"You do, do you?"

"Yes, she was at home."

"You were there with her?"

"Not exactly." She closed her eyes.

"Define 'not exactly,'" Agent Jackson said.

Talia took a deep breath. She fought the urge to throw up and then she pressed on. "I was sitting in my car in front of her house."

"What were you doing in your car?"

"Watching her house."

"Stalking her?" His voice contained a tone she thought sounded just shy of amused.

"Not exactly." Before he could ask for another definition, she added, "Okay, yes, I was kind of stalking her."

"Why?"

"Because she fascinates me?" It came out as a question, much against her will.

"I need your name, miss."

"Do I have to give it to you?"

"How else can we verify your story?"

"My name is Talia. Can you keep this information confidential? God, I would be so embarrassed if anyone found out."

"Your last name?"

"Lisher," she said, then spelled it out for him.

"Well, Miss Lisher, don't you think we would be remiss if we didn't inform Ms. Eliot that she had a stalker?"

"I—ah—I guess."

"Now, why should I believe you and not think that you're making it up to help out a friend?" Jackson asked.

Talia thought hard. Of course they would be suspicious of a sudden alibi. "I can tell you that Shay's neighbor three doors down sneaks in and out of the house next to Shay. Each night at just after midnight the guy goes through the side door and stays at least an hour."

"Hmm," was all Jackson said.

"Shay's next-door neighbor on the other side walks her three dogs, one at a time, to the corner and back. She starts after midnight and takes them each out for about ten minutes. She never picks up their dog mess." Then she remembered something that could be corroborated. "She ordered a pizza on Saturday night, and oh, on Friday night, there was a traffic stop on the street that runs parallel to Shay's. I suck at directions, but it would be to your right if you were facing Shay's house on the opposite side of the street."

"What time was that?"

"At one twenty that morning." She remembered being scared to death that they would come down Shay's street next and catch her there. "Oh, I guess that would have been technically Saturday morning. You could ask the Norfolk cops about that, right?"

"I will do that. I need a telephone number to call you back if I have any further questions."

She gave him her number and he ended the call by telling her to quit stalking Shay Eliot.

"Yes, sir," Talia responded.

†

Shay opened her front door to let Kate and Lana in. "You will not believe this," she said. "Apparently I have a stalker and she can vouch for me being home the two nights I couldn't account for."

"Oh, that's great," Lana said, all but jumping up and down in her delight. "I mean, not the stalker part, but you know...Who is it?"

"Her name is Talia Lisher. She's the young woman with all the hair and—"

"Oh no," Kate said. "That's not good."

"What are you talking about?" Lana said. "That's very good. Now they will leave Shay the hell alone."

Shay studied Kate's expression. "What's wrong, Kate?"

"I know Talia. We went to high school together, but she was one grade ahead of me. She's a Liarhead Lizard. Once the FBI figures that out, it's going to look like you put her up to it."

47

"What the hell is a Liarhead Lizard?" Lana asked.

"That was the nickname for her and her older brother. They were notorious liars when we were growing up."

"A lot of kids lie," Shay said, still hopeful.

"They took it to a whole other level. It was like a sport for them or an art form. For example, Talia and Brian told a neighbor, who was new to the area, that they'd seen a man kidnap a woman at gunpoint and take off in a boat on Chisman Creek. The neighbor didn't know their reputation so he called the police. They refused to admit to making it up and gave statements to the cops and everything." Kate started pacing. "She could have made things worse for you."

Shay sat on the edge of her sofa and put her head in her hands. "It can't get much worse." Then the image of Diane's body in the backseat of the car slammed into her mind. She felt ashamed for a moment for losing perspective. She was alive. Allie and Diane weren't.

"Maybe the FBI won't find out about Talia's history with lying," Lana said.

"I could wait and see what comes of it," Shay said. "Or I could tell the FBI I've just learned of Talia Lisher's history and assure them I didn't ask her to lie for me."

"I vote for leaving it alone," Lana said.

She looked from Lana to Kate and back to Lana. She thought about that day three years earlier, when Kate was looking like a viable suspect in Lana's boyfriend's murder, and Lana gave Kate an alibi. Shay hadn't thought for even a moment that Kate had killed Richie, but her superiors and colleagues sure did.

Shay didn't know what to think. She'd been so excited about having an alibi. Now she didn't know what to do. She would rather leave it alone, but knew she should be proactive since this was so serious. "Damn it," she muttered.

†

Talia was on edge at work the next day. She kept expecting the FBI to show up at the dentist's office to question her. Dr.

Bennett would have a field day with that, she was sure. But no one came in, no one called, and Talia had no idea if they would follow up on what she'd told them or not.

She couldn't help but wonder if the FBI would connect her name to Brian's, since he was in a federal prison. Would they think that if one sibling was an embezzler maybe the other also was capable of doing horrible things? Sometimes Talia got very angry that Brian got into trouble and other times she just felt sorry for him. She missed him and loved him but felt more at ease without him around.

Talia had worked herself into a nervous knot by the time she made it to the bar that night. She was so upset she couldn't eat dinner before going out and knew she wouldn't be able to eat once she got there. Her nerves wouldn't let her.

The woman at the door waved her through. Talia had been there enough over the last several months that she guessed she was officially considered a regular.

Talia turned toward the dance floor when she heard Kate call out, "Eliot, wait."

But Shay Eliot wasn't waiting. She was making a beeline right for her. Talia was scared and excited all at once.

"Outside. Now!" Shay barked.

Talia almost tripped trying to keep up with her. Damn, and no drink yet either.

"What the hell were you thinking?"

That wasn't what she was expecting to hear. Maybe, *quit stalking me, loser*, but not that.

"What do you mean?" Talia asked, her voice quivering.

"Do you have any idea how bad it's going to look for me when they look into your story? Seriously, what were you thinking? You have to retract your statement. You aren't even a credible witness, for crying out loud," Shay said.

All Talia could think to utter was "What?"

"Come on! Kate told me about your problems with not telling the truth. She told me about you and your brother sending the cops on a wild goose chase after some guy with a hostage—a story that

turned out to be fabricated. She told me about your nickname—
Liarhead Lisher—"

"Lizard. It's Liarhead *Lizard.*" Her face was so hot she
expected to break out into some kind of hives. "You're going to
judge me based on some adolescent crap years ago?"

"I'm sorry, but I don't believe you were sitting outside my
house two nights in a row. And when the FBI proves that you lied,
it's going to make me look bad. They're going to think I put you
up to it."

"They are going to check out my story and you will be off the
hook. They aren't going to give a shit if I told lies for attention
when I was younger."

"Stop it," Shay said through clenched teeth. "Stop the crap
and don't try to help anymore, okay?"

Talia could feel her fists clenching and unclenching by her
side. She knew she should say screw it and leave, but she couldn't
stop herself. "So, Shay Eliot, did you know that it's your neighbor
to the right letting her dogs shit in your yard without cleaning it
up? Huh? How about the neighbor on the other side of you? Did
you know she entertains another neighbor after dark?"

Shay looked confused and said nothing.

"Am I a freak stalking you? Yes. Am I a liar? No—not in this
case anyway, not about where you were those nights. Oh, and you
ordered a pizza from Calz's on Saturday night."

"I—ah—"

"So, if it's all the same to you, I won't be retracting my
statement to the FBI. And maybe one day when you pull your head
out of your ass you'll thank me for coming forward."

Talia marched toward her car, not allowing herself to look
back. She peeled out of the parking lot and drove two blocks
before stopping on the side of the road. She looked around
thoroughly, double-checked that her doors were locked, and sat
there for a while and cried.

Eventually, she put the car back in Drive and headed home.
She cranked up the music, singing along to Sam Harris's
"Pretender." She loved the sound of the song, but the words
always made her uncomfortable. Weren't pretender and liar the

same thing? Weren't she and Brian pretending to be needed when they lied and told the police they saw the man with the gun? And wasn't Brian just pretending more by adding the detail about the kidnapped woman?

When "Over the Rainbow" started she hit the eject button on her favorite cassette and wondered if she'd ever be able to listen to it again without it bringing memories of the murders and Shay's reaction to her.

Talia felt sick. She always did when she thought about making stuff up. The worst part was that the kidnapping story wasn't even the biggest lie she'd told. She cringed as she thought about the time Brian had told her to tell their parents that her female gym teacher, Ms. Simmons, had touched her down there. "Teach the dyke a lesson," he'd said. But Talia couldn't bring herself to do it, even if going against her brother scared her. So she'd run away and was gone for three days. She'd broken into the Cunningham place. The house, a few miles away, had been empty since the old couple died several months earlier. She'd eaten some food she'd brought with her and some canned ravioli she found in the cupboard. When she finally went home she weaved a fantastical story about Gypsies and amnesia. Brian was so impressed by her intricate storytelling that he left her alone about the gym teacher.

But even that wasn't her worst lie. No, that distinction went to the lie she told when she was thirteen and her dad died. She'd put it to words though, and now she could never change her story—not even to Brian.

Chapter Five

Every time Shay thought about how she spoke to Talia Lisher her face heated up and her stomach churned. Who had she turned into?

"It's Liarhead *Lizard*!" Talia had shouted at her. The look on Talia's face was one of shock and guilt and something else. What was that look, exactly?

Shay thought about seeing Talia around the bar over the course of several months. She'd always found her attractive, but she was younger, like Kate, and a bit on the wild side, unlike Kate. And what in the hell was Shay doing comparing Talia with Kate?

She'd spoken briefly with Talia right after Allie and Diane were murdered. Talia seemed so vulnerable that night, when everyone was shouting their opinions about what had happened on the parkway. The young woman had seemed almost like she was in shock. So much so that Shay was surprised when Talia said she didn't know Allie and Diane.

Shay wanted to ask Kate more about Talia, but she wasn't sure Kate could be objective about her. For some reason, the mere mention of Talia's name put Kate on the defensive. Shay wondered if there was more to their history than Talia's reputation for lying.

Shay went into the garage and moved everything from in front of the punching bag. She started hitting it and her head cleared a little. She should talk to Talia, apologize for acting the way she had. Or not. Maybe she shouldn't do anything to encourage the young woman. The last thing she needed was to give her the wrong idea but, she pounded the bag faster and harder, she did owe Talia an apology. She would tell her she was sorry the next time she saw her at the bar.

After showering, Shay dressed in black jeans, a white T-shirt, and tied the laces of the black Reeboks she thought of as part of her security uniform. She might as well be comfortable standing around both inside and outside the bar all night. So far there had been no trouble, thank goodness. She pulled on the dark blazer and checked that the gun in its shoulder harness wasn't too obvious. She knew most folks at the bar knew she would be armed, but didn't want to flaunt it.

Once at the bar, Shay went inside. She leaned against the corner between the front door and the bar area and sipped a glass of water. There were a few people in there, even though it was still pretty early. She helped Dee change out the keg then went outside. Almost immediately, a squad car pulled up beside her.

"Hey, Parker." Shay squatted beside his car.

"What's up, Eliot?" He looked her up and down. "What are you doing out here?"

"Checking out the parking lot."

"Working security?" His eyebrows knitted together.

"People are more than a little freaked out after what happened to those two women on the parkway."

"I heard about your interview," he said, his voice low.

"You mean my interrogation?"

"Must have sucked. Especially since you knew the one."

"The *one's* name is Allie. And a lot of women around here knew her. People are scared."

"I can understand that. Please be careful out here."

"Of course." She leaned closer. "So, Parker, what are they saying? What do you hear about the murders?"

"Not much. Since it was on the other side of the water and is a federal thing, we don't hear a lot. Well, just that part about you," he said.

"I guess all the guys think the traitor ex-cop dyke deserved to be dragged into this mess, huh?"

"Well," Parker stammered. "There will always be some assholes in the department. But we aren't all like Dixon and McCoy, you know," he said, referring to the two officers who'd beat up Paulie.

"I know," Shay said.

"And I hated how you were pretty much pushed out."

So that's what they are calling it. It wasn't lost on her that he didn't hate it enough at the time to have her back. But she had to move beyond that. "Thanks, buddy. I need to go check the back of the parking lot."

"Okay. If I do hear anything I'll let you know."

She nodded. She didn't know how much she believed that, but appreciated the sentiment.

†

Talia was checking her mail in the bank of boxes when she felt as if she was being watched. She looked behind her and saw her neighbor from across the parking lot, the one she was still mentally calling Maybe Lesbian. "Hi," Talia called out.

"Hi." The woman walked up and stuck her key in her box. She pulled out a stack of junk mail and said, "Killing all those trees for this." She tossed it all into the can available for that.

Talia held up her electric bill. "Trade you," she teased. She decided to hang around a few moments so she could check the name on the newly trashed junk mail, but Maybe Lesbian didn't seem in a hurry to go anywhere, so Talia said goodbye and walked back to her apartment.

Talia locked the door behind her and grabbed her notebook from the kitchen counter. Pen in hand, she settled in front of her makeshift coffee table. She wanted to put together the right words to describe how devastated she was by Shay Eliot's rejection, but she felt numb.

She thought about the literal image of a lizard. Some lizards changed color for camouflage but were hiding in plain sight. Was the murderer of Allie and Diane hiding in plain sight?

What if it was a cop or a park ranger? She tried to count the number of times she'd been on the parkway with a group of friends and was approached by a ranger. On senior skip day they all went to the beach area off the parkway, the place they called Sandy Point, to party. They'd eventually been run off by the rangers, and a few of them even had their beers poured out and were given a warning to go right home.

Lately there had been some talk that the parkway was a gay hangout. Talia guessed she was just oblivious because for her it had always been about partying. Except for that one time, five years earlier, just after Talia turned eighteen. Talia had known her whole life that there was something different about her, but didn't know what. Then she had met Bernie at the beach in Yorktown and gone parking with her at the parkway. It had been Talia's first time with any woman, and the only time with Bernie. At first, her feelings had been hurt when Bernie hadn't called like she said she would, but she got over it, and was thankful that she finally knew why she never wanted any of the boys in the neighborhood to grope her.

She was very thankful that she'd never done that on the parkway again. She cringed every time she thought about how, if the killings were a random act, it could have just as easily been her or any of her high school friends that were killed.

Would the women of the bar be mourning Talia if it had? Don't go there, she told herself. And what if she went out there now? She could get a gun and sit out on the parkway to wait for the murderer to come to her. Then she could win everyone's admiration for solving the crime.

Talia turned her attention back to her notebook. She sketched a lizard on the blank page. Even though she sucked at drawing, sometimes when she couldn't make the words flow a little visual stimulus would help. She stared at the lizard. Liarhead Lizard, Liarhead Lizard, Liarhead Lizard, she repeatedly thought of the hated nickname.

Think of a lizard's parts, she told herself. The tongue tastes and smells? They have eyelids, whereas snakes do not, right? She tried to remember if they were scaly. And she'd seen for herself that as a defense mechanism, the tail would come off if they were caught by it.

Talia squeezed her eyes shut. There was a poem in there but she couldn't make the words come. Instead, her mind kept going back to how angry Shay was when she told Talia to take back her statement, and she kept reliving the sick feeling in her gut every time she thought of Shay's words, *Stop the crap.*

Talia's eyes teared up. She had lost any chance at getting to know Shay. She was way too embarrassed to ever show her face at the bar again. And even though she now knew the parkway was a gay hangout, she couldn't go there after what had happened to Allie and Diane.

She jabbed her pen into the lizard drawing again and again, striking harder and harder each time. Liarhead Lizard. Then she was assaulted by the image of her unresponsive father in the bathtub. He was bluish-white and bloated as Talia stepped back and shut the door to the bathroom, going back to her bedroom to pretend she hadn't seen anything.

Talia hurled her pen across the room. She didn't deserve a new poem. Or Shay Eliot. Or anyone for that matter.

†

Shay checked her watch before dialing the number that FBI agent Nathan Jackson had given her. She wanted to talk to him about Talia Lisher. She had been glad that it was Jackson who'd called her about her alibi and not Timothy Grainger. She knew Grainger had been doing his job, but would never feel he had the right to talk to her the way he had. But mostly, she hated him for showing her the gory pictures that still haunted her nights.

Agent Jackson answered the phone. She asked him if there was anything new and when he said no, she believed him.

"Should I be worried about this woman, Talia Lisher?" she asked.

"Ah, your stalker." The agent laughed. "It appears she's just a bit lovesick. We've checked her out and there is nothing on her personally. Her brother is a different story, but Talia Lisher appears to be harmless."

"Okay, I just wanted to be sure."

"You want us to have a conversation with her?" he asked, his voice all but mocking.

"No, it's not necessary. I'll handle her."

They hung up and Shay was pretty sure she wouldn't be hearing from the FBI on this matter again. She hoped they would do the investigation justice. Allie and Diane deserved that.

Now to figure out what to say to Talia and how to do so. Talia hadn't been back to the bar since Shay had yelled at her. Shay knew she could make use of her investigative skills and find out how to reach Talia, but wasn't quite sure what she would say once she did.

†

Talia held the white plastic suction tip in place in Mrs. Robbins's mouth as Dr. Bennett drilled the decayed portion of one of her molars. As long as she could keep the woman from gagging, this part of her job was what she called a no-brainer.

She stared at Mrs. Robbins's ear for a long time before she realized it was a bit misshapen. Talia allowed her thoughts to drift. Words presented themselves, taunting her, teasing her when she couldn't write them down.

"Talia," Dr. Bennett said.

She knew right away she'd let the suction tip drift out of position. "Yes, sir," she said, repositioning it out of his way.

Van Gogh's ear. On this woman. Talia caught herself smiling. If Van Gogh's ear had ovaries…

It wasn't until two patients later that Talia had a moment alone with her thoughts and a small notepad she kept hidden in her smock pocket. *Van Gogh's ear and a wolf. No, fox. Coyote. Yes, coyote.* She jotted down some thoughts, hoping she'd be able to remember the rest and put it all together into something meaningful once she was home.

Talia's workday was coming to a close and she was loading dirty instruments into the autoclave when Lacey came up behind her. "I keep forgetting to ask you about your costume party."

Talia shook off the image of the two women dressed as Allie and Diane with their throats slit. "It was great. I won first prize with my mummy costume." And there it was…Liarhead Lizard…slipping out…easier than the truth… "And good thing they did the judging early in the night because I was afraid to pee until afterward. I knew I'd never get rewrapped as well as what you'd done." Talia smiled, and then excused herself. She hid in the bathroom the last ten minutes of the day, waiting for Lacey to go to her car ahead of her.

When she finally went out into the parking lot, she stopped short just outside on the sidewalk.

"I almost didn't recognize you," Shay said.

Talia hadn't even thought about how different she would look to people outside of the bar.

"No mascara, hair not styled," Shay explained.

Talia's face warmed; she didn't know which embarrassed her more, the version of her standing in the parking lot in a smock covered with cartoon teeth, hair pulled back, no real makeup to speak of, or the person Shay saw at the bar, hiding behind makeup and teased hair.

Shay must have sensed her discomfort. "You look cute in real life."

"Thanks," Talia said. "I think." She took in the sight of Shay—beautiful in a pair of dark jeans and a light blue polo shirt that matched her eyes perfectly.

"So, I came by to thank you. You know—for helping me out. But mostly to say that I'm sorry. I acted abominably."

"Abominably. That's one hell of a word," Talia said.

"Too much?" Shay asked.

"No, quite fitting actually."

Shay laughed. Talia found it to be a glorious sound. And then it sank in. Shay Eliot had sought her out. Shay stood in front of her, looking amazing, and apologizing.

Talia didn't know what to say or how to act. Surely Shay didn't drive all that way just to say thanks and sorry. "Would you like to do something?" Talia glanced down at her smock and scrubs bottoms. "After I change, that is."

"Yes, I would," Shay said. "I'm parked over there—the tan—"

"I know."

"Oh, yeah, you do know what I drive."

"I'm the silver Honda," Talia said, feeling pretty lame.

Fifteen minutes later they were in Talia's apartment. She never in a million years imagined she'd be showing Shay Eliot around her place. In all her fantasies they danced and kissed at the bar or made love at Shay's house. But here Shay was, standing in front of Talia's ugly plaid sofa, near her homemade cinder-block-and-ply-board coffee table, looking around the room without any outward signs of judgment.

"I'm going to change real quick." Talia practically ran into her bedroom. She closed the door behind her and leaned against it. *Get it together*, she told herself as she took several deep breaths. She slipped out of the cheesy smock and scrubs Dr. Bennett made them all wear and into a pair of worn, faded Levi's. Then she slipped on a T-shirt and hoped she didn't look too casual. She was about to throw her smock in the hamper when she remembered her notebook. The coyote and Van Gogh had to wait, she thought, as she put the notebook on her bedside table.

"Can I get you something to drink?" Talia asked as she came out of the bedroom. "I have soda, beer, and juice."

"I'll take a soda."

"I was going to order pizza. But we could have something else if you'd rather." She held up a Jolt and a Coke by way of offerings.

"Coke would be great. And pizza sounds terrific." Shay looked around the room. "This is a nice apartment."

Talia wanted to act like a normal person who had normal friends come over to hang out with her in a normal way, but this was all so foreign to her. She usually went to old high school friends' places to get stoned, or went out to the bar to be around

other women like her. She wasn't sure how to be a hostess.
"Would you like to see the rest of the place?"
"I'd love to."
At least Talia had been raised to keep things clean and neat.
She thanked God she wasn't a slob who'd be embarrassed now.
She led Shay down the hallway and pointed out the bathroom.
"Do you live alone?" Shay asked.
"Yeah." Next she pointed out her bedroom with its small bed
and single dresser. Clean, but by no means fancy. Or very adult,
she suddenly feared.
"This is nice," Shay said.
"Here's the spare room."
Shay stepped into the room this time. "Wow. This is very
cool." She stood in front of the canvas with "Soul Dancing" that
Talia had just hung. Shay's lips moved slightly as she read it to
herself. Talia wanted to touch those lips with hers so bad it hurt.
Then Shay stood in front of "Taste," and Talia read it to
herself as Shay did the same.

I lean into you, pressing you into the wall. My tongue curls
Around a strand of your hair, a trace of raspberry. I breathe
The earthy freshness of your green apple soap. Arranging
My mouth on yours, a mint-tinge of toothpaste screens
The delicate subtlety of dinner's chardonnay. I brush
My lips against your salt-laced neck. Gripping
A piece of you between my teeth, you taste
Sweet and sour. I hold on, afraid to lose
The power of jalapeno masquerading
As refined vanilla.

Shay blushed slightly and Talia knew she was turning red as
well. The scent of raspberries filled her head and she feared Shay
would know the poem was about her.
The doorbell rang and Talia was glad to get Shay away from
her poems. She couldn't believe she'd let her read the ones she did.

Shay was the only person who'd read them and that both thrilled and terrified Talia.

Shay smiled when the pizza delivery guy addressed Talia by name. "You order pizza as much as I do, I see."

"Yeah. When I'm not eating Taco Bell."

Shay laughed.

They made their plates on the kitchen counter then Talia led the way into the den. Shay sat on the end of the sofa and Talia sat on a hand-me-down La-Z-Boy chair her mom left with her when she moved to Pennsylvania with her new husband to start their new family.

They said little as they ate, but it was comfortable. After eating, Talia got Shay another soda.

"Can I read more of your poem paintings?"

Talia was surprised. And pleased beyond what she was sure was warranted. "Sure."

They returned to the poem room. Shay stood in front of "No" and read this one out loud.

> "No, I don't hate men
> and no, I was never
> abused and no, I am
> not going through a
> phase and no, it isn't
> about finding the right
> man and no, I'm not
> confused and no, I
> have not been
> indoctrinated and no,
> it isn't about anything
> other than loving
> Women."

"I could see this on the wall at the bar," Shay said, pointing at 'No.' "I'd bet they'd buy one from you. I could see it written on a red background and hanging between the pool tables."

61

Talia had no idea how to respond.

"You do sell your work, don't you?" Shay asked.

Your work. The words flew around her mind. Shay said it like Talia was a real artist and not the hack poet she knew herself to be. "Yeah," she managed to say, "I do sell my work." Not really a lie, because she would if she could, right?

"I'll see what I can do," Shay said.

The phone rang, but Talia stayed where she was, staring at Shay and thinking about what a terrific day this had turned out to be.

"Are you going to answer that?"

Talia looked at her watch. Seven p.m. It would be Brian. She couldn't talk to him with Shay there. It eventually quit ringing.

"So, I was going to ask you for your phone number, but it appears you don't answer your phone."

Shay was saying she wanted her number? "I usually do answer my phone."

It was Shay's turn to check her watch. "I should probably get going."

"Okay. Let me get something to write with and I promise I'll answer your call if I'm home." Talia grabbed a charcoal pencil off the drafting table in the corner and ripped off a little piece of sketch paper. After she jotted down her number, she handed it to Shay.

The phone started ringing again. "I should get that," Talia whispered.

"I can let myself out," Shay said.

Talia walked with her to the door. She grabbed the phone just before she knew it would stop ringing and answered the question asked immediately with, "Yes, I will accept the charges." She wondered if Shay heard that as the door shut behind her, and if so, what she'd think of it.

"Hi, Tali. What's shaking in the land of the free, kiddo?"

"Hi, Brian."

"When you coming back to visit? I'm dying for some more baby back ribs."

Memory of the heat of the ribs as she wrapped them with Saran wrap to try to keep the smoky-sweet scent hidden and then taped them to her torso rushed over her. "I'll try to come this weekend. But I can't bring you ribs again."

"Ah, come on."

"No, Brian. I was scared to death I'd get caught. And I flat-out lied when they asked me if I had any weapons, food, or beverages on me. I lied to federal cops."

He let out a big, full-bodied laugh. "Now you're worrying about lying? Oh, Lord, what has happened to you?"

A lot, but she wasn't telling him that. She wasn't going to tell him about how she'd been working really hard on not lying or embellishing. She also wasn't going to tell him about the van on the parkway, or the two women being murdered. And she was going to keep to herself how she finally got to spend some time with Shay Eliot. This was her life, separate from her family, and she wanted to keep it that way.

"You still there?" Brian asked.

"Yeah, I'm here. Sorry, but I can't sneak anything else in for you."

"It's all right. I just want to see you. The ribs were a bonus. How's the Honda?"

"It's good."

"You're still taking good care of it?"

"Yeah," Talia said.

"Not tempted to trade it in, are you?"

"No, I promised you I wouldn't."

"Good. So, how's your love life?"

Talia hated when he pressed her about that.

"You seeing anyone?" he asked.

"Yeah. A guy I met through work." She rolled her eyes at herself. "He's really nice. And has a good job. And great teeth."

Brian laughed. "As long as he has good teeth. What's his name, I want to check him out for you."

She knew she had to stay with the lie. She didn't know if he could actually check on her story from inside prison. "You know I can't say anything else about him. Patient confidentiality," she blurted.

There were voices in the background, getting louder.

"Sorry, kiddo, but my phone time is up. I hope you do come see me this weekend."

"I'll try."

"Tali-ho," he said, his usual way of ending the conversation.

Talia hung up and felt guilty. She wasn't totally convinced she would try to see him that weekend. Going to the prison made her very uncomfortable. She knew it was a minimum security place, and that it was all white-collar offenders there, but that didn't make her feel much better.

She went to the stereo and hit the play button, and Patsy Cline's voice filled her apartment. She was glad Shay hadn't asked to play some music because she would have been embarrassed, considering the whole stalking thing and all.

In the poem room, Talia placed a canvas on the easel. She took out the red paint and the motion of applying it to the canvas helped her to relax. She would do several coats, then wait a day or two before adding the words. The lettering would need to be heavier than usual since the background would be darker than what she typically worked with.

She sang along to "Crazy" and felt like new and wonderful things were beginning to happen.

†

Shay walked the periphery of the bar's parking lot. So far the only incidents she'd had working bar security was with the local, young homophobes. Nothing new there. She was hoping to be able to get one of them to stand still long enough to talk to him, but as soon as they knew she was on to them, they'd take off, leaving behind the echo of gay slurs. She believed a few minutes talking to them could help educate them. Or not.

She scanned the parking lot for Talia's silver Honda. Shay had been thinking a lot about her. She wanted to spend more time with her, but also wanted to be sure it was done very slowly. On the other hand, she wished Talia wasn't quite so young, and she wasn't quite sure of her intentions or her past history, as explained by Kate. She did like her, though, and had enjoyed spending the time with her when she'd gone to apologize. She just wasn't sure if she should get close to someone who seemed as wild as Talia did at times.

Movement near the road caught her attention. One of the local teens that she'd seen before was skulking along the side of the road, a bulky down coat making him appear bigger than what she imagined he really was. He was looking in car windows. Maybe now would be her chance to talk to one of these kids, get them to see her and everyone else there as humans to be respected, not tormented.

Shay stayed close to the building, out of the light of the streetlamp, and watched him. He appeared to have something in his hand. She could make out the outline of a large piece of a broken cinderblock. Keeping out of the light, she made her way along the row of parked cars between her and the street. She knew this would be the time to call out, and he would drop the cinderblock and run. But she kept quiet as a rage pulsed through her. How dare this punk kid come here and even think about doing damage to one of these cars?

Once she was within a few feet of him, she stepped out into the light of the streetlamp. Simultaneously, he had raised the cinderblock over his head, over the windshield of a brand-new Ford Taurus.

"Hey!"

He jumped, dropped the block, and moved as if to flee. She grabbed him by the bulk of his coat and swung him around.

"Get your hands off me, dyke."

"Who the hell do you think you are, coming over here, trying to damage people's property?"

He jerked out of her clutch. "I haven't done anything. And I ain't scared of you, you ain't no cop."

Shay pulled her jacket to the side, just enough to expose her holstered gun. "For you, I'm worse than a cop. I'm a big, mean dyke who doesn't give a crap about 'protect and serve' when it comes to loser punks like you. Come around here again and I will show you how fed up I am, and how much I don't care about laws when it comes to protecting the people and cars around here." She glared at him. His eyes kept moving to the gun still showing. "Now get the hell out of here!"

He ran. He didn't look back.

She stepped to the side of the building and took several deep breaths, trying to calm herself. It wasn't lost on her that a learning moment was missed with that kid. And it wasn't lost on her that she didn't care. She was so mad, so tired of people thinking it was okay to do harm to the cars in the parking lot of a lesbian bar.

Dee came out the door to the parking lot and lit a cigarette. Shay walked over to her.

"That shit will kill you," Shay said, getting herself together.

"And so will so many other things—and people," Dee said.

"You feeling a little morbid tonight?"

Dee took a long drag. "I can't shake the looking-over-my-shoulder feeling. You don't think it could be someone we know, do you?"

It bothered Shay that she knew without her saying that she was talking about Allie and Diane. So many people were thinking about what had happened. "I sure as hell hope not."

"Some of the regulars aren't coming out anymore. They'd rather stay home or have parties at different women's homes. Business being down hurts financially, but what's even worse is knowing that people you care about are scared."

"Yeah. I feel so helpless in this whole thing." And she did. At least while she was a cop she had some resources available to her and she was somewhat in the loop about what was going on in town.

"There is something you can do—we can do," Dee said.

Shay looked Dee over carefully. Her friend had a thinking-way-too-hard expression on. "Should I be afraid?"

"I've had several women tell me they think it'd be a big help if women felt more empowered."

Shay couldn't argue with that, so she didn't. "Okaaaay?"

"And we think if you taught self-defense to whoever was interested that would help," Dee said.

"There are people a lot more qualified to do that than I am." She snatched the new cigarette Dee was about to light out of her mouth. "Besides, I don't have any place to teach."

"Sure you do." Dee grabbed at her cigarette but Shay was too fast. "You can teach right here, during the day. We could set up a weekday afternoon class and one on the weekend."

Shay thought about that.

"And you *are* the most qualified because everyone here trusts you and respects you," Dee said.

"We would need some supplies. Mats for starters."

"You tell us what you need and we'll get it. Figure out how much you want to charge. You can keep all the fees. And we'll make money on drinks and food because folks will need some nourishment after kicking your ass."

Shay smiled. "Sounds like you've thought this through."

"I think it'll be good for everyone. You in?"

"I'm in." Shay handed the cigarette back to her. "Isn't your break over?"

Dee laughed. "Coming in?"

"No, I had to scare off a punk intent on mischief. I think I'll hang out here for a while longer."

An hour later, Shay felt pretty sure the kid wouldn't be back, so she went inside. She leaned against the wall and watched the women. It was fascinating to look around at all the different types of people who came together under one roof. Some women held court at tables, letting people they knew come to them, others milled about, going from table to table, or perhaps conquest to conquest.

A woman danced slowly alone on the dance floor, oblivious to anyone else. At times she closed her eyes, other times she watched herself in the mirrored wall. She was a good dancer, maybe a little too gyrating at times for Shay's taste, but good nonetheless.

Someone she recognized from her cop days came out of the bathroom, swiping at her nose. Shay had no doubt that she and the other woman who came out immediately after her had been in a stall snorting. Not my problem, she reminded herself. She was just there to keep everyone safe.

The music changed and "Like a Virgin," came on. The lone dancer started moving as if acting out the words of the song. Shay stared for a few seconds, then looked away. She saw Dee standing, frozen, at the bar, her face pale. Several other women had similar expressions. Shay felt a bit ill as she remembered the AIDS fundraiser they'd had at the bar the year before, when Allie had lip-synched to that song, also acting out the words.

Suddenly the music ended and a faster dance song came on. Shay realized Toni was in the DJ booth, just as she had been the night of the fundraiser. Toni would know what painful memories would be provoked by watching that woman act out the song exactly as Allie had.

Chapter Six

Talia's good mood from spending time with Shay kept her high the entire next day. Then something amazing happened. Shay called her Friday evening and invited her to dinner at her place for the next night.

Talia spent most of Saturday trying to decide what to wear. She thought about what Shay had said to her in the parking lot outside of work. *You look cute in real life.* What if Talia showed up in little makeup and unteased hair and Shay decided she liked the bar look better?

Shay hadn't really noticed Talia with all the hair and makeup prior to her coming out as her stalker, so maybe she should try the other look for this dinner. What could it hurt? It would cut down on the time it took to get ready and it would cut down on the upkeep throughout the evening. And what if Shay invited her to spend the night? Waking up with makeup smears and huge bedhead was not a good look for her.

Talia decided to wear minimum mascara and a touch of lip gloss. She wouldn't give herself big hair, she would just let it feather away from her face with no hairspray or mousse. She put on an emerald-green blouse and black jeans. Finally, she slipped into her black loafers.

As she was heading out, she saw her notebook and thought about the poem she'd started. She grabbed her larger notebook and the small one with the notes jotted in it, and sat on the bed. Before she knew it, she had a first draft.

Van Gogh's Ear

If Van Gogh's ear
grew ovaries,
and lay with an androgynous coyote
on a bed of pine cones,
then birthed a kit one year later,
suckled by a black bear,
mentored by a lioness,
finally named Myself...
seeking,
searching,
always listening,
Van Gogh's ear with ovaries.

She was happy with it as a start and thrilled that she'd done it without a ton of caffeine or any speed.

Even though she already felt jazzed from writing, Talia knew she'd need a little caffeine to stay energized. She sipped on a Jolt Cola on the drive to Norfolk. Luckily, the tunnel hadn't backed up yet, or was in between backups. Talia was just glad not to be sitting there for any length of time getting her blouse wrinkled. Even though it was cool out, she kept the AC blasting to keep from sweating too much from nerves.

As she turned onto Shay's street, Talia wondered if she should have brought something. Wine? Flowers? No, not flowers. Crap. She didn't even know the basics about lesbian dating. There were a lot of cars on the road in front of Shay's house. Talia almost drove past as she realized it wasn't a date but a gathering of friends.

Friends.

She parked but stayed in the car for a few minutes. Then she realized that was like stalking. She had to decide: go in and be one in a group of her friends, or leave.

Talia got out of the car, locked it behind her, and marched toward Shay's house before she could chicken out. Shay met her at the door, saying, "Hey, you made it."

"Hi," Talia said.

"Come on in. You know a few of the women here, but let me introduce you to the rest."

She followed Shay into the kitchen where Kate and Lana were working by the stove. "Hi, Talia," Kate said, not overly friendly.

Lana turned and reached out her hand. "I don't believe we've been properly introduced. I'm Lana Christianson."

Talia shook her hand. "Talia Lisher."

"Can I get you a drink?" Shay asked. "Beer, soda, some booze?"

"A soda is fine for now."

Shay handed her a can of Coke and grabbed her glass off the counter. "Come on outside and I'll introduce you to everyone else."

There was a swirl of names and small talk before Talia ended up at a picnic table with Shay.

"You look great today," Shay said.

Talia's eyes made their path over Shay's body before she could stop herself. Shay was wearing a white button-down shirt with dark blue jeans. "So do you," Talia murmured. She looked around the backyard. "This is an awesome yard."

"Thanks." Shay sat on the bench beside Talia. "We're having hot dogs and burgers. Is that okay?"

"Sounds great. Smells great."

"It does. Ginny's cooking because I've been banned from the grill. Last time we had a cookout I burned up the first batch of food and someone had to take over." She grew somber. "Wow, I'd forgotten. It was Allie who did the grilling after I ruined it."

By the look on Shay's face, Talia knew which Allie she was referring to. Talia couldn't imagine how hard it would be to hold that kind of memory after someone you knew died, especially if they died at the hands of someone else.

"I'm sorry," Talia whispered.

Shay clapped her hands once, as if snapping herself out of a bad dream. "Today is a day to celebrate."

"Did someone say celebrate?" A woman whose name Talia had already forgotten approached them.

"Yes, Brit, someone did," Shay said as she lifted her glass. "Here's to old friends and new."

Talia nervously touched her soda can to Brit's beer bottle and Shay's cocktail.

"So, Talia, I hear you're from the other side of the water."

"Yes. I live in Newport News now, but grew up in Seaford."

"Oh, Kate grew up in Seaford, didn't she?"

"Yes," Talia and Shay said simultaneously.

"Well, we like pulling our *family* over to our side," Brit said with a smile. "So, Shay, I hear you agreed to teach self-defense at the bar."

"Yeah. We thought at first we'd start with two classes a week, but now I'm thinking we'll start with one a week, on Saturday afternoons, and see how it goes. There are still a lot of details to work out."

"I think that will be great," Talia said.

"Yes, anything that involves sweating women is bound to be pretty great," Brit said. She looked at her empty beer bottle. "Time for another beer. Check you later."

"You doing okay?" Shay asked Talia.

"Yeah." She looked around at the small groupings of women around the yard. "This is nice." And it was nice; even if it wasn't the intimate dinner she had thought it would be.

"The food should be ready soon," Shay said.

Talia was surprised how relaxed she felt. When she pulled up and saw all the cars, she thought for sure she would feel uncomfortable around Shay's friends, but she wasn't. It was a big plus that Shay was sitting with her, talking to her, acting a little like her date.

"We have to make sure you get some of the baked beans. Dee sent them over even though she couldn't make it since she's working the bar tonight."

Talia looked more closely at the corner of the yard. There was a lawn mower and other lawn care equipment. She remembered the talk that Shay was doing landscaping now that she had quit the police force.

"Do you miss being a cop?" Talia asked.

"Yes and no. My answer to that question seems to depend on what day it is."

"Why did you quit?"

"I guess I'd become disillusioned. Jaded."

"Someone at the bar said it was because one of your cop friends beat up a queen you know."

Shay nudged Talia's knee with hers. "You believe everything you hear at the bar?"

"No." She shrugged. "Hell, I don't even believe everything I hear out of my own mouth."

Shay let out a huge laugh and most of the women in the yard turned to look in their direction. Talia felt a sense of pride that she'd made Shay laugh and that everyone saw them sitting together.

"Come and get it," Ginny hollered.

"Chow time," Shay said as she stood.

As everyone fixed their plates, lanterns started to come on, adding a soft glow to the yard. Talia hadn't noticed them hanging from trees around the yard. It was such a cool touch.

Talia felt a little chill when she sat beside Shay at the picnic table. Kate and Lana sat opposite them. Talia noticed Lana had slipped on a jacket and decided after she ate she would go to her car to see if she had a sweater or jacket in the backseat.

About halfway through the burger and beans on her plate, Talia started to shiver but thought she'd hidden it well, so she was surprised and grateful when Shay got up to get them each a vodka and tonic and returned with a jean jacket too. She handed it to her and Talia warmed from the gesture. She grew warmer still at the way the scents of raspberry and vanilla came from the jacket. "Thank you," she managed to get out.

"You're welcome. If that doesn't do the trick we can move inside. I just thought it was too pretty of a night to not take advantage of it."

"It is beautiful out tonight." Out of the corner of her eye Talia saw Lana nudge Kate. Talia found herself not caring what that was about. She was sitting beside Shay, eating a perfectly grilled burger, and wearing a jacket that smelled like Shay. It was a beautiful night, all right.

"So, Talia, how's your brother doing?" Kate asked.

She didn't know what Kate thought she was going to accomplish, or what game she was playing, but Talia was beyond caring. "He's doing great. As a matter of fact, I'm going to visit him tomorrow."

"Oh?" Kate asked.

Brit had just sat down on the end of the bench next to Talia. "Where's your brother live?"

"Brookeville, at the federal penitentiary there." There it was, out in the open. Welcome to Talia's world, warts and all.

Brit almost spit out a mouthful of beer.

Shay squeezed Talia's shoulder. "I think it's good you see your brother."

Talia leaned in to Shay's touch and was disappointed when Shay removed her hand a few moments later. She could tell Shay already knew about Brian being incarcerated. Of course, Kate would have told her all about Talia's messed-up family. She wondered what else Kate had told her. Talia looked across the table at Kate. She could have easily asked Kate if April was still clean, but she already knew the answer to that one. At that moment, she actually felt sorry for Kate. Talia didn't care how many degrees in psychology Kate acquired, she still came from a family as messed up as Talia's.

At least Talia had the class to keep her judgments to herself.

†

Talia walked slowly across the parking lot to the entrance of the prison. She felt guilty even though she wasn't doing anything wrong. She wasn't trying to sneak anything in, and she wasn't going to lie about anything. So, why did she feel so anxious?

The guard barely looked at her as he asked about food, weapons, or any other contraband. As he led her to the main room with tables and chairs spread throughout, she saw Brian immediately. His hair looked shorter than she'd seen it since his trial and the goatee he had grown was also gone.

He gave her a bear hug before letting her sit down, then told her all about his new job coaching one of the softball teams. It felt more like camp than prison, except for the part where Brian wasn't allowed to leave, all the windows had bars, and the guards at the gates wore big guns.

She told Brian he looked good and he told her she did as well.

He looked over his shoulder, pulled her close, holding her hand on the table and said, "Kind of bow your head a little. Make it look like we're praying."

Talia tried to pull away, but he held her there. "Come on. The guards love this shit."

"Brian, really?" she whispered. "I think faking it is a bigger sin than not doing it at all."

"This isn't about sinning. It's about how the guards treat the guys who are into God better than they treat the rest of us." He winked at her before saying in a much louder voice, "Amen."

She felt a little sick. Pretender. Liarhead. "That's just not right."

"What's not right is me in here and people who did a lot worse than me are still out there. What's not right is my own sister won't even sneak some ribs or BBQ in here for me."

Talia stood up to leave.

"Sit back down. I'm sorry. Come on."

She sat. She didn't always like her brother, but she did love him. People change when locked up. She bet Kate Hunter could tell her all about the psychology behind that.

"Tell me about work," he said, "and about the new boyfriend."

She told him a few stories about dirty mouths and scared patients. One old man had locked himself in the bathroom because he didn't want a root canal. It took an hour for his wife to talk him out. He left without the procedure.

Talia noticed that Brian kept looking over her right shoulder as she spoke. She turned to see what he was looking at. At the table behind them, a young man and woman sat close, holding hands and talking. They looked utterly sweet and in love.

"And the guy you're dating?" Brian asked.

"History," Talia lied. "He wasn't really my type and I got bored so I broke up with him."

"Do I need to arrange retaliation against him for anything?"

"No, don't worry. *I* broke *his* heart." She wondered if he could reach out and touch someone from inside the prison. She looked him over. He smiled at her and she thought no, he was all talk. That was probably how he handled being incarcerated, by trying to feel like he was still in control of his life.

"That's my girl."

Talia turned to look again when Brian's attention drifted back to the table behind her. The man caught them looking and turned abruptly away. When Talia turned back to face her brother, she couldn't help but notice the I'm-up-to-something smirk on his face.

Usually on her way out she tried hard not to look at the others, but couldn't help herself. She always just wanted to see how scary they really were. A few looked like trouble, but mostly they looked like the normal people they were. Normal people who, for whatever reason, had broken the law. She knew Brian was there because of greed, but imagined some of the men were there because of crimes they committed out of desperation. Sometimes people did bad things when they were hungry or had lost hope.

This time, Brian insisted on walking her to the door leading out of the large visiting area. He stopped at the table with the young couple. "Hey, Rob, I see your bride came again to see you."

Rob seemed to tense, and his wife looked confused.

He said to Rob, "This is my sister, Talia," and to Talia he said, "this is Rob, my neighbor." Brian used his 'plotting' voice.

"Hi," Talia said, feeling uncomfortable. She looked into Rob's eyes for a long moment, imagining how cool it would be if she could telepathically send him a message to watch out for Brian. She turned toward the woman and said hello to her as well, even though no attempt was made to introduce her.

When they moved again toward the door, Talia made small talk. "They look like a sweet couple." She wondered if Brian would tell her what he was up to.

"Sweet couple, huh?" He shot them a glance. "That's his sister-in-law. Rob's in here for insurance fraud related to his wife's death. They couldn't pin the murder on him, so they went for the easy win with fraud."

So, she thought, the bride comment was a taunt.

"When Rob and I get out of this dump, we're going into business together."

"Oh," she took the bait. "What kind of business."

"Life insurance, of course."

At the door, Talia gave her brother a hug. He said, way too loud, "God bless you, Tali."

She hurried past the guard he was trying to impress. When she got to the car, she opened the door and the smell of BBQ sauce assaulted her. She glanced down at the ribs wrapped in plastic wrap. She hadn't been sure if she'd leave them behind or not until she got to the prison. She'd thought about Shay then, and how Talia was pretty sure they'd be over before they even got started if she'd been caught breaking the law.

Leaving the prison grounds, Talia forced herself to drive the speed limit until she got to more familiar territory. Once on Route 17, she pulled into the Texaco gas station and threw away the ribs, then drove with the window down, trying to get the smell out.

Several miles later, she looked into her rearview mirror in time to see a dark blue van cut across two lanes of traffic to get in the right turn lane behind her. She rolled up the window and floored it, pulling out in front of a Ford Maverick, the driver let her know his displeasure with a horn blast and hand gesture that involved one finger.

Talia sped down Ft. Eustis Boulevard until she realized she was leading her pursuer to her place. That was the last thing she wanted. Instead of turning left on Jefferson Avenue, she went through the light and got on I-64 heading toward Norfolk.

Glancing in the mirror, Talia noted the driver of the van had a ball cap pulled down low on his head so she couldn't make out his face. He stayed right with her as she weaved through cars. What her Honda didn't have in power it made up for in heart, and she was in flight mode. Each time the van managed to maneuver around cars with her, she was shocked and more afraid.

When she saw the sea of taillights ahead of her she didn't have enough time to get in the right lane to jump off the interstate at LaSalle Avenue. Now she was stuck. Crap, crap, crap. There was a cop in traffic about four cars ahead of her. She vowed that if she saw the van's door open she would get out and make a run for the police cruiser. She undid her seat belt just in case. When she remembered the open bottle of schnapps under her seat and the weed in her glove box, she decided the cop would be the very last resort.

Traffic started to creep again and her heart sank as the cop got off the interstate. But, the cars were moving again. They got up to about forty mph through the tunnel, then it all opened up and Talia was able to go sixty on the other side.

The van stayed right with her. She drove like a maniac, occasionally getting some distance between them, but then inevitably some pokey jerk would get in her way. By the time she exited at Chesapeake Boulevard, she didn't see the van. She floored it to the intersection at Five Points and made a hard right onto Sewell's Point without waiting her turn. She ignored the honking horns and jerked the wheel left into the bar's parking lot. She slammed on her brakes and skidded up to the door, blocking in several cars where she stopped.

Cindy was checking IDs at the door and Talia ignored her pleas to move her car. There was no way in hell she was going back out there.

"Is Shay working?" Talia shouted.

"Day off." Cindy pointed toward her car. "Move your car, please."

"It's an emergency. May I use the phone please?"

Cindy rolled her eyes and nodded toward the office door. Talia was pretty sure she thought it was just some more garden-variety dyke drama and not a life-and-death situation.

Talia dialed Shay's number from memory. "Shay, I'm sorry, but I didn't know where else to go or what else to do—I didn't tell you or anyone, else but one night on the parkway I was chased by a van and today it followed me to Norfolk, and maybe even to the bar."

"Are you sure it's the same van?"

"Positive. Shay, I'm scared. What should I do?"

"Stay inside the bar until I get there."

"I'm blocking people in."

"Find Dee and put her on the phone."

Talia did as Shay asked. When Dee hung up and came out of the office, she looked serious. "Want a drink, Talia?"

"No thanks."

"Well, that's a first," she said.

Talia shrugged.

Shay came into the bar fifteen minutes later. On her way to the phone in the office, she muttered, "I miss my police radio." She picked up the receiver from the office phone and punched in a number. "Parker, I need something, buddy." She paused as he spoke, then added, "Because you're the only cop in town still speaking to me." She laughed. "And because I'm so charming. I need you to run a tag for me. It's for a blue Chevy G20 van." She read it off. "This is extremely urgent." She gave him the number she was calling from, said thanks, and hung up.

"He'll call me right back," Shay said to Talia.

"You got the tag on the way in?"

"Yes."

"So he is out there," Talia said.

Shay nodded.

Dee brought Shay a soda, and then turned to Talia. "Tina needs to leave. May I move your car?"

Shay held out her hand and Talia handed her the keys. When Shay came back in several minutes later, she said, "The van is gone."

The office phone rang. Shay answered it, obviously comfortable taking charge. "Hey Parker, thanks." She jotted down some information. "If it turns out to be anything, I'll give you a call first." She hung up.

Shay turned to Talia. "Jeffrey Gardner. Sound familiar?"

She shook her head.

"He has a Yorktown address and a record for possession."

"I think I'll take that drink now," Talia said.

"How about you hold that thought. Let's go to my place and you can tell me the *whole* story."

Talia nodded.

"We'll take your car and leave my truck here. I can come back for it later."

Talia followed her out and realized Shay had put her T-shirt on inside out when she'd rushed to Talia's rescue. Her breath came faster and she felt a little woozy. No wonder she had fallen hard for this woman.

Shay turned and looked at her. "You okay?"

"Your shirt is on inside out."

She looked down and laughed. "It sure is. Now you see me for the bum I really am."

Oh, I see you, all right. "Thanks for coming to my rescue."

Talia drove toward Shay's house. They both kept looking around. "Do me a favor—pass the house, go around the block, and then come back."

She did. Shay seemed to think it was okay. She got out, opened a gate in the fence, and had Talia pull into her backyard.

"Your lawn—" she protested.

"It's fine. It's safer this way. Just don't go doing any doughnuts back here," she teased.

She shut the gate and they entered the house through the patio door.

"Now for that drink," Shay said as she went into the kitchen. "Your usual okay?"

At the word *usual*, Talia smiled. "Yes, thank you."

Talia's smile disappeared when Shay came into the living room with a serious expression. "You need to tell me everything and with total honesty."

She bristled, even though she knew she deserved that. Talia told her about the van chasing her on the parkway, and about how she wasn't sure of the color. And about seeing the black van at the scene when the bodies were found and how that had freaked her out.

"You should have come forward with that."

"I was scared to death. And with all the talk that it might have been a cop that killed Allie and Diane, I didn't want to tell the wrong cop." Talia gulped her drink. "This van was obviously blue. I'm pretty sure the van at the scene was black. And I know the body bags were white." She shuddered.

Shay took her hand. "Why didn't you tell me about seeing all of that?"

"I didn't want to come across as wanting attention. Not after all that had happened."

Talia jumped at a noise at the patio doors. Shay got up and went to the door. After looking out, she slid the glass open. A scrappy, skinny tabby cat came waltzing in. "This is Poke," Shay said. The cat came over, sniffed Talia's shoe, and then went into the kitchen. "I found him a few years ago on the road into Poquoson, on my way to the seafood festival. He was so small and scared, I said screw the festival and came home with him instead."

Talia should have known Shay was a cat person. Talia loved cats but didn't trust herself to have that much control over another life.

"I wanted him to be a housecat but we couldn't make that work. So he comes home most nights and I don't lecture him too much about running around."

"He's handsome," Talia said.

Shay finished her drink before setting the glass on the coffee table. "We need to talk about sleeping arrangements."

Talia almost spit her drink across the room.

Shay laughed. "Don't worry, I won't hold you here against your will but I do think it's a good idea for you to stay here. You can have the guest bedroom and I will have peace of mind that you aren't out getting yourself in trouble with men in dark vans."

She'd always dreamt of spending the night with Shay Eliot, but this was not how it went in her fantasies. "Okay," she agreed.

✝

Shay is running down cobblestone streets lined with trees, stopping every few yards to look in car windows. All along the side of the road cars, trucks, vans all sit idle, waiting for her. She takes deep breaths before peering in each window, afraid of what she might find. In every vehicle, the seats are bloodied, but no one is there. Finally, she gets to the last car. She doesn't want to look in, but she does. Talia's bloodied body is in the driver's seat, and someone is on the floor of the passenger seat. The glove box is opened and its contents are scattered about, some papers stuck in the blood covering the woman. She is convinced the person is Allie, until she turns and faces her. Shay sees herself staring back, her throat slit, her mouth half-open, trying to say something.

Shay jerked awake from the nightmare and sat up in bed, panting, thrashing her way out of the binding of the sheets around her ankles. Tears came. She thought about getting up to get a drink of water, or a beer, but then remembered Talia in the bedroom next door and decided to stay in bed. She didn't want Talia to see her like this. She glanced at the clock. Five a.m. She would lie there and wait for a more normal hour.

At eight o'clock, Shay was in the kitchen scrambling eggs when Talia came out of the spare room. Talia gestured toward the phone on the wall. "Mind if I use the phone to call into work? It's long distance."

"Go ahead. You going in late or taking the whole day off?"

"Think I'll take the whole day." She dialed the number and left a message. As soon as she hung up the receiver, the phone rang.

Shay reached for it. "No," she said into the receiver. "I don't get the paper anymore since I'm, ah, self-employed." She gave

Talia a little grin. "What?" The grin disappeared. "Wow. No, I hadn't heard anything." She started spooning eggs onto two plates then added some bacon from a plate lined with paper towels. "Sure, come over. Bring the paper with you."

"Sorry about that," Shay said to Talia. "First, you do eat bacon and eggs, right?"

"Yes," Talia responded, "and second?"

"That was Lana. We're having company in about twenty minutes. A woman's body was found in the York River last night. I'm not sure if they've been searching the river all this time looking for evidence in Allie and Diane's mur—" She stopped short, fighting to tamp down the image from her nightmares. "I don't know why they were looking in the river, but the newspaper said the body had been there a long time."

"What does that have to do with…oh crap," Talia said.

"Lana said Kate immediately went to a dark place and is sure the body is her mom's. Apparently after studying about postpartum depression, she's convinced not only that her mom had it all those years ago, but that April has it now too."

"April?"

"Yeah, she had a baby about six months ago. You didn't know? I thought all you Seaford kids knew everything about each other."

"Yes, but so few of us live in Seaford anymore." She took a bite of eggs and groaned her satisfaction. "So Kate thinks her mom is dead?"

"Yeah, she thinks she committed suicide back when they were younger, after she left them."

"Huh."

"Huh, what? You look deep in thought."

"It's just that my mom told me once—granted it's been a while—but she told me she ran into Mrs. Hunter in Pungo once or twice."

"Pungo?"

"Yeah, you know, near Virginia Beach. They have the strawberry festival there every year."

"I know where Pungo is, but would Kate's mom be that close and not be in touch with her family?"

The doorbell interrupted them.

Kate's eyes narrowed when she saw Talia. Lana raised her eyebrows and smiled.

"Talia had a situation last night and we decided it was safer for her to stay here," Shay said.

"I can go get cleaned up in the other room while you talk," Talia muttered.

"Actually, Talia, can you stay here a few minutes?" Shay looked at Kate, then Lana. "Talia was telling me something pretty interesting."

Talia shrugged.

Kate handed Shay the newspaper. Shay read the article, and then handed it to Talia.

"Sometimes, you just know things." Kate stood with her arms crossed over her chest, daring them to say otherwise. "The paper says the body has been there for a long time and that it looks like a probable suicide. My mom was depressed for a long time before she disappeared."

"Tell her what you told me," Shay said to Talia.

"My mom told me she saw your mom in Pungo years after she left. She was at the strawberry festival. Your mom was working it, not visiting."

"Pungo? You can't be serious."

Shay gave Kate the look she usually saved for people sitting in the backseat of her squad car. There was no way she was going to let Kate start in on Talia about the liar stuff.

"Well," Talia said. "My mom is a Liarhead Lizard, so..."

Shay laughed.

Kate looked sheepish. "I sounded so disbelieving because when I think of Pungo I think of rednecks or druggies, and well, my mom was neither."

"I can't even say for sure my mom was telling the truth, but it could be worth looking into."

"I could ask around," Shay said. "I have some friends in Pungo. Friends who are neither redneck nor druggie," she teased.

"There is something else," Talia said to Kate.

"What?"

Talia hesitated.

"Seriously…it's okay…tell me," Kate said.

Shay studied Kate, and Kate's expression softened, looking more like Shay imagined Talia would remember her from high school.

"When April had that issue with drugs, well, my mom said something about the acorn not falling too far from the tree. I figured she meant something about your mom and drugs," Talia said.

After some discussion about Talia's revelations, Kate said she and Lana needed to leave. Before they did, Shay agreed to take a trip to Pungo in the next day or two.

As soon as Shay and Talia were alone, the phone rang. Shay listened intently, then said a few okays and yeses before hanging up. When she got off the phone, she told Talia that Parker had made some inquiries based on what she'd told him the night before, and the van at the scene on the parkway was black and belonged to the funeral home. They had been called to remove the bodies and transport them to the crime lab.

"Now at least we know the vans aren't connected," Shay said.

"I can't wait for this whole thing to be figured out and for someone to pay for these murders."

Shay nodded. "A lot of people will feel much safer then."

Chapter Seven

Talia was in the lab area pouring a stone model for a patient's crown. She held a finger between the metal tray of impression material and the top of the vibrator to buffer it a little. She started the flow of stone mixture from one end of the tray and let it go in slowly, being careful to vibrate out any bubbles as she went to keep the model from having voids. Dr. Bennett hated voids. She stared, loving the lava-like viscous flow of the mixture.

She smiled at the memory of when the last vibrating thingamajig had conked out and Dr. Bennett asked her to order a new one. Sally usually did the ordering but was on vacation. Talia had no idea what was the official term for the thingamajig and was mortified when she called the dental supply company to order a new one. Talia and the rep on the other end of the phone laughed for ten minutes about Talia wanting a new vibrator for work. In the end, she got the equipment Dr. Bennett wanted, but still didn't know it by any other name.

Dr. Bennett was in the hallway talking to a patient and Talia heard them mention the woman found in the York River. She took the tray she was pouring stone into away from the vibrator to better hear but only a few words made it to her, and she was risking screwing up the model so she quit trying to eavesdrop. Maybe Lacey was hearing the conversation and Talia could ask her later.

Talia finished pouring the model and was quite impressed by her work. It wasn't lost on her that the parts of her job she enjoyed the most didn't directly involve patients. More than once she'd thought that maybe she should look into working at a dental lab.

At the end of the day, Talia and Lacey were in the lab area. As Lacey cleaned the counter space and Talia pulled sterilized instruments from the autoclave, she asked, "Did you hear what Mr. Wilson was saying about the woman pulled from the river?"

"Yep." Lacey came closer. "Definitely looks like a suicide. Been there so long it may be tough to get an identity. They're looking into a few possibilities. You know, women who went missing from the area a long time ago."

Women like Mrs. Hunter, Talia thought. She found herself wondering which would be harder, finding out your mother killed herself years earlier or never really knowing what happened to her.

She was still thinking about the Hunters when she left for the day and walked into the parking lot. That's one of the reasons she jumped when she saw April Hunter standing next to her car.

"Hi, Talia."

"Hey, April. What's up?"

"Please tell me you have something. Anything." She leaned closer as she spoke.

Talia grew concerned that April might raise her voice. It'd be just Talia's luck that she'd say something about drugs loud enough for Dr. Bennett to hear on his way out. "I have a little weed at the apartment."

Talia had enough for about a joint. And then that was going to be the end. She was going to quit smoking pot all together. She didn't like doing it enough to risk news of it getting back to Shay, or getting caught with it, or being tempted to cruise the Colonial Parkway looking to score from Fish. No, after this little bit, she was done.

April followed Talia in her little Ford Pinto, parking a few spaces down from her and trailing after her into the apartment.

"Want something to drink?"

"Got a beer?" April asked.

Talia handed her an Amstel Light and opened a Jolt Cola for herself.

April kept leaning as if to see out the kitchen window as Talia rolled the joint. April was making her feel paranoid and she wasn't even buzzed yet.

"Everything okay?" Talia asked.

"Yeah," April said. "Everything is fine."

Talia fired up the joint and handed it to her. Talia didn't really feel like smoking so she took tiny hits and kept passing it back to April. Talia wished she had given it to April to take with her.

April closed her eyes and inhaled deeply.

"Do you know who Jeffrey Gardner is?" Talia asked.

April exhaled hard. Her eyes sprang open and she looked thoughtful. "Yeah, I know Jeff. Why?"

"How do you know him?"

"He and Boyd used to hang out every now and then." April averted her gaze when she said Boyd's name. Talia couldn't help but wonder if she still loved him a little, even though he was a hoodlum and had caused all kinds of turmoil for April and her sister.

"Really?"

"Yeah. Boyd and Jeff used to hang with your brother Brian too."

Now she really had Talia's interest.

"I remember the first time I saw them together it surprised me because, at that time, I thought Brian was in no way a thug like Jeff." She took another hit off the joint, breathed in deeply, then let it out slowly. "What's it say that it didn't surprise me that Jeff and Boyd were hanging out, huh? Maybe deep down I always knew my boyfriend was a thug."

Tears flowed down April's face, coming faster and faster, but she didn't make any noise or act like she even knew she was crying. She cried like someone who'd done it a lot lately. Talia decided if April wasn't going to acknowledge the tears, she wouldn't either.

She put the last of the joint in the ashtray. April looked around the room and Talia got up to get her a box of tissues. April blew her nose on one, then shoved some extra tissues into her pocket.

"Boyd was afraid of Brian," April said. "I never did understand that."

"Afraid of Brian? Really?"

"Boyd didn't admit it, but the way he tiptoed around your brother always made me wonder."

Talia stared at April. Someone like Boyd Smith—someone capable of murder—was afraid of Brian? She couldn't quite wrap her head around that, and it nagged at her.

"I better get going. Thanks for the buzz," April said.

"You should probably know that I'm not getting any more weed. Or speed."

April nodded and headed toward the door. Talia watched from the door as she walked to her car. She leaned into the backseat and pulled something out.

Talia gasped when she saw her holding her six-month-old baby for a moment before putting him back in the car. Talia wanted to throw up. Her hands shook as she went back into her apartment. She emptied the ashtray of ashes and the roach into the toilet and flushed it. Then she leaned over the sink and threw cold water on her face.

Talia had to do something. Or tell someone. She had to tell Kate. Or she could tell Shay and have her tell Kate.

But what would Talia tell Shay? What would she say they were doing in her apartment while the baby was in the backseat of April's car?

How about the truth? she thought. Yeah, Lisher, that would be nice. Tell the truth.

Talia jumped at the knock on the door. She peeped through the hole and saw it was April, with the baby this time. She opened the door and April asked if she could change the baby's diaper in the bathroom. Talia stepped aside and she came in.

Before she could shut the door, Talia saw Maybe Lesbian wave to her. She waved back, then shut the door quickly behind her. She grew paranoid about what Maybe Lesbian might think of her, if she would figure out why April was there. *Oh, stop*, she told herself. *It's the pot making you paranoid.* She turned her attention back to April.

She wondered where April's husband was. It flashed through her mind that maybe April would leave the baby behind. No, she was stoned, not crazy. Well, maybe not crazy. What was it Kate was saying about postpartum depression? Talia quickly regretted the little bit of weed she did smoke. Her mouth was dry and she wasn't sure how to handle a depressed new mother.

April came out looking better than when she went in. "I gotta big case of the munchies. You got any Doritos?"

"No, but I have Fritos." When she started to pout, Talia added, "And some mild Taco Bell sauce."

"Make our own Doritos? Now you're talking."

Talia got out the chips and sauce and grabbed two Cokes. Now that she knew April had the baby with her, Talia wouldn't even offer a beer. They started shoving the food into their mouths. Talia wanted April to keep snacking until the buzz wore off.

The baby made a few baby sounds.

Talia dipped a corn chip into the taco sauce. "What's the baby's name?"

"Joseph. After my husband, Joey."

She saw the opening. "Where is your husband?"

"He works a lot of hours these days. At the shipyard."

Talia nodded.

April held up a Frito and asked Joseph, "What's this?"

"Futc."

"That's right, it's a fucking Frito." She held up her lighter. "What's this?"

"Futc."

"Correct, a fucking lighter."

"Futc!" the baby said louder, and then laughed.

Talia had to laugh too. Maybe she wouldn't have found it funny if she hadn't had a buzz, but April was laughing and Talia couldn't help thinking that was a good thing, all things considered, so she laughed along with them.

"At least his first almost-word is a fun one," April said.

Talia was glad to see April enjoying herself, but couldn't help but feel like the kid was going to have a rough time of it if April didn't get some help.

When April and Joseph left, Talia felt a little better about April driving with the baby, but knew she still had to say something to someone about her leaving him in the car for the amount of time it took them to smoke the joint. And when Talia did say something, April would hate her and Shay would be disappointed in her, but she would at least know she did the right thing by speaking up.

✝

Talia's vision adjusted to the dim lighting and her eyes were drawn immediately to where Shay sat at the bar. Her heart pounded as Shay turned to face her. She imagined maybe Shay felt her presence and that's why she turned when she did. That's what Talia was hoping, anyway.

"Hi," Shay said as Talia came up beside her.

"Hi." Talia motioned to the chair, still not wanting to assume too much.

"Sit. Can I buy you a drink?"

"Vodka tonic would be nice." Talia looked around. Lana was working, but she didn't see Kate. "Is Kate around tonight?"

"No, she's home studying for a big exam coming up next week." Shay swiveled around on her barstool and smiled at her. It was the most gorgeous thing Talia had ever seen. "You tell me about your last couple of days, and then I'll tell you about my trip out to Pungo."

Talia didn't want to tell her about April yet. She would do it; she just didn't want to start the evening with that. "No, you tell me about Pungo first. It's not fair to make me wait to hear about that."

Shay smiled again. "Okay, guess I'll be nice and not keep you hanging." She took a sip of her drink, then told Talia about talking to some folks who remembered a woman who called herself Karen Stephens. She fit Karen Hunter's description, showed up at the same time Mrs. Hunter disappeared, and had left with a man a couple of years earlier.

"So she's gone?"

"Yeah, but I have the man's name and know enough about him that I should be able to find him. His family's from Roanoke Rapids. He's a plumber, and his name is Winston."

"That's some pretty specific information."

"Yep. So, I'm thinking about a trip to North Carolina tomorrow. You want to come along and see what we can scare up?"

"I'd love to." Going on a weekend day trip with Shay Eliot was about the best thing she could have hoped for. "Wow. This is so cool."

Shay signaled Dee for another round. "Now it's your turn."

"Can we get a table in the corner?"

"If you want." Shay cocked her head and studied her for a long moment. When Dee set their drinks down, Shay picked them both up and led the way to a relatively secluded table.

Talia didn't waste any time once they were seated. "I saw April the other day."

"You did?" Shay sat back and crossed her ankle over her knee, in an ultra-relaxed pose. "When I first met April Hunter she was a scared sixteen-year-old trying to act like a grownup. Then she got her act together and turned into a lovely young woman."

How did Talia tell her that she saw the scared girl again? That she was actually afraid for April's baby?

"When's the last time you saw April?" Talia asked.

"Oh, it's been a while. Back when she was pregnant, probably around six months along."

Shay leaned forward and asked, "What's up, Talia?"

"Please hear me out before you pass judgment."

"I'm hurt that you think you have to start any conversation between us like that."

Talia stared at her. She could tell Shay really was hurt and that made her feel like crap. "I'm sorry. It's just that this whole honesty thing is new for me. And telling you the whole story and not picking and choosing the details makes me feel vulnerable."

"Come on, spit it out." Shay reached across the table and grabbed her hand. The sweetness of the gesture almost made Talia cry.

She told Shay about April coming over and getting stoned together. Shay kept a steady, expressionless look on her face until Talia told her the part about the baby being in the car the whole time. "I swear to God I didn't know the baby was in the car. The thought never even crossed my mind. I mean, who does that?"

"Then what?" Shay said as she pulled her hand away from Talia's.

"Then she came back in with the baby and we pigged out on junk food."

Shay massaged her temples.

"The whole thing kind of freaked me out." Talia looked at her hand and wished Shay hadn't let it go. "And I want you to know that the pot we smoked was the end of it for me. I'd already decided not to smoke anymore."

"Tell me more about your time with April," Shay said, dismissing her claims of getting cleaned up. "How did she seem when she left?"

"She seemed better. At one point she was crying but never said exactly why. I assumed it was because we were talking about Boyd."

"Why in the hell would you be talking about Boyd?" Her voice rose for a second, then she calmed down. "What the hell?"

"I asked her if she knew Jeffrey Gardner and she said he was friends with both Boyd and my brother." She experienced the same dizzying sensation she felt every time she tried to imagine Brian hanging out with people like Jeffrey and Boyd—Boyd was a murderer for Christ's sake.

"What?"

Talia nodded. "I didn't know my brother even knew Boyd, let alone hung out with him."

"Hmm. That's interesting." She seemed to think about that for a few moments.

"Look, I'm sorry about getting high with April. That's not going to happen ever again. I'm sorry I made her cry. But what we need to be focused on is the fact that she has got some serious issues."

"Postpartum depression," Shay guessed.

"You think?"

"Could be."

"Can I still go with you tomorrow?" Talia asked.

Shay stared at her for several moments. "You don't have any drugs on you right now?"

"No, and there are none in my car. And none at my apartment."

"You promise you won't ever have any drugs around me?"

"I promise."

"Well then, I guess once again we need to talk about sleeping arrangements. I want to leave pretty early tomorrow so you should probably stay at my house tonight so we can leave from there. Is that okay?"

Okay? "Couldn't be better." She studied Shay from across the table and thought about hearing her nightmares the last time she spent the night in Shay's spare room. She wondered if that was a recurring thing and if it had anything to do with the murders.

✝

Shay was driving Talia's car because the bed of her truck was loaded down with lawn care equipment. They were on Highway 58, not too far from Emporia, where they would pick up I-95. Shay kept catching Talia watching her hands on the wheel.

"What are you thinking?" Shay asked.

"Nothing," Talia said.

Shay could see Talia's blush move up her neck to her face. She smiled, wondering if she'd caught Talia having intimate thoughts. If so, then so much for total honesty. But, in Talia's defense, Shay knew some things just needed the right time and the right place to be discussed. She wondered if they'd ever find that place and time. Every time they were around each other, Shay thought that would be the time she would finally kiss Talia. But then, it wasn't.

"What else did April say about Jeffrey Gardner?" Shay asked.

"She said he was a thug."

"And they all knew each other," Shay said.

"Yeah. I don't know what the connection would be. Brian is a white-collar criminal. Not that it's any better, but it doesn't really make sense that they would be in business together."

Shay pulled into a gas station. "I'll get gas while you go to the restroom, then I'll take my turn."

Talia was waiting in the car when Shay got back in. Shay handed Talia a Jolt, and the smile she got in return made her grin back. The act was so familiar that it made Shay's stomach do a little butterfly flip.

Their next stop was at a gas station in Roanoke Rapids. They found an ad in the phone book there for a Winston Plumbing Company. They drove to the address and weren't surprised the building was closed up for the weekend. There was an on-call number stenciled to the glass door, but Shay wanted a face-to-face with the guy first.

"How do we find where he lives? We don't even know if Winston is a first or a last name," Talia said.

They rolled down the windows and Shay sat completely still for a while, then suddenly sat up straighter and smiled. She started the car and followed the dirt drive back behind the plumbing business. The path curved around and they saw a mobile home tucked between the trees.

"How did you know this was back here?"

"I didn't, not really," Shay said. "I remembered how that gas station we stopped at earlier had a driveway going back behind it. While I was pumping gas, I saw one of the attendants drive behind the building and figured maybe he was going home for lunch. At the time I thought, how convenient."

"And maybe Winston the plumber likes things convenient as well."

"We're about to find out." Shay nodded toward a man in jeans and a dirty T-shirt working on an old Ford. She pulled up behind the Ford and said to Talia, "Look confident. Shoulders back. Handshake firm."

Talia followed her as she approached the man. "Hello, sir, my name is Shay Eliot." She held out her hand and he shook it. "I'm looking for Winston."

"I'm Winston." He looked at Talia.

She followed Shay's lead and stuck out her hand. "I'm Talia Lisher."

"What can I do for you ladies today?"

"I'm a private investigator, and I'm looking for Karen Hunter," Shay said.

He cocked his head and studied her. "I don't know any Karen Hunter."

"Don't you live here with your girlfriend, Karen?"

"Yeah, but her last name is Stephens."

"We have reason to believe her real name is Hunter."

"You got you some bad information, I'm afraid."

"Karen Hunter lived in Seaford, Virginia, until 1971."

"You got the wrong Karen." He took turns cracking the knuckles on first one hand, then the other.

Shay noticed a subtle change in his demeanor. "I don't mean to bring y'all any trouble, it's just important that I at least talk to Karen Stephens to make sure she isn't also Karen Hunter."

"I'm sorry, but I can't allow that. Karen is under the weather and won't be seeing you today. Or any day. Please, you've got the wrong person. Just leave."

"Can you say beyond a shadow of a doubt that your Karen isn't Karen Hunter?"

"Well, I can say that if she was and wanted me to know about her past she would have told me."

"Kate Hunter thinks a body they pulled from the York River is her mom," Talia blurted. "She thinks her mom suffered from postpartum depression and killed herself. And she's afraid that her sister, April, is following in their mom's footsteps."

"I feel bad for your friends," Winston interrupted. "But Karen was sick. And now she's doing pretty good and I'm not gonna let anyone or anything drag her down to that dark place she was in when I first met her." He scuffled his foot in the dirt. "I'm sorry, but I ain't taking any chances."

Shay pulled out a piece of paper and pen. "Here's my number. If you change your mind, please give me a call."

"Give him mine too," Talia said. "And write my first and last name. Mrs. Hunter was always so nice to me when I was little."

Shay finished writing and handed the paper to him. "Karen Hunter has two wonderful daughters and a beautiful new grandson."

They got back in the car and started down the dirt drive. "Do you think we'll hear from him?" Talia asked.

"I don't know. I think he's too scared."

"Scared of what?"

"Losing the love of his life to her past."

"So you do think we got the right person?" Talia asked.

"Yes, I do."

They rode in silence until Shay pulled onto the interstate.

"That was a nice touch, the lie about being a private investigator," Talia said.

"I'm not sure it was as much a lie as a proclamation."

Talia turned in her seat to face Shay. "You thinking about becoming a PI?"

"I do seem to have a knack for finding people."

"Yes, you do. And that would be very cool."

Shay smiled and for a moment forgot that even though they'd found Winston, they still didn't know for sure if they'd found Mrs. Hunter or how they would actually get her to talk to them.

"What will you tell Kate?" Talia asked.

Shay shrugged. "I don't know."

✝

"Wow," Talia said as she approached Kate, standing beside her car. "I never know who will be waiting for me out here after work."

"Can we talk?" Kate asked.

"Sure." Talia knew she needed to face this head-on. "I was going to stop at Taco Bell on my way home. Interested?"

"Who doesn't love Taco Bell?" Kate said, obviously trying to keep things light.

"We can go through the drive-through, then you can follow me to my place."

Twenty minutes later they had settled on each end of the sofa with their food and drinks on the rough planks of Talia's coffee table. They took turns commenting on their appreciation for Taco Bell as they ate. After washing down her last bite of burrito, Talia asked Kate, "You're here to talk about April?"

"Shay told me what happened when April came by to see you." She took a sip of her drink. "April's had a really hard time since having the baby. I knew she was depressed, but hadn't realized she started doing drugs again."

Talia felt compelled to respond in some way, so she nodded.

"Do you know how bad the drug thing has gotten?"

Talia thought about that. "If she was using a lot she would have some kind of connection. But each time she's come looking to me for drugs she's been pretty desperate."

"So, you've gotten high together more than once?"

Total truth, Liarhead, she told herself. "No, only that one time. Another time—on Halloween—I saw her at the store and she was looking for some speed. I told her I didn't have anything."

"Why has she started looking to you for drugs?"

Talia held up her hands. "Look, I'm no dealer or anything. I think maybe she just doesn't know where else to look, her connections have all dried up. Or maybe I'm safe. Hell, she's a lot better off coming to me to smoke some weed than hanging around downtown Hampton or cruising the parkway."

When Kate turned pale at the mention of the parkway, Talia regretted her words.

"The parkway—is that known for drug dealers?" Kate asked.

"It's not a big thing. It just happens to be where I find mine. Maybe she doesn't even realize that's an option. I sure as hell don't plan on telling her."

"I don't know what to do with her," Kate whispered.

"Have you thought about spending more time with her?"

"What's that supposed to mean?" Kate bristled.

"Don't get defensive on me," Talia said. "It's just that when we were hanging out I got the feeling she was lonely. Joey's been working a lot of hours. Maybe she needs some company."

"School is kicking my butt. Other than chilling out at the bar an hour here and there, I don't really have any spare time."

"Maybe you need to find the time. Or have Lana spend some time with April. Or volunteer to take Joseph overnight sometime so April and Joey can have a date night."

Kate leaned forward and rested her chin in her hands.

"Maybe some weekend Shay and I can hang out with them. Or take Joseph for an evening."

Kate's eyes narrowed in the manner saved for any time Talia and Shay were in the same location or sentence.

Okay, no more easy-does-it. Talia was getting irritated with that look. "And quit with the evil eye. Shay and I are spending time together, like it or not."

She sat up straighter. "Oh, so now you're seeing each other?"

"I didn't say that."

"What are you saying?" Kate asked.

"I'm just saying that you're with Lana, but you seem to have this sense of possession over Shay. It's like you don't want her but you don't want anyone else to have her either."

"That's absurd," Kate said.

"Is it? You kind of like having a backup plan in case things don't work out with you and Lana, don't you?" Her voice rose with every word and she didn't like it. She took a deep, slow breath. "I'm sorry. I know you don't want Shay and I to be together, but I really like her. And it's okay if she doesn't feel that way about me, but it's not okay if you try to sabotage her happiness out of some perverse jealousy."

"I am not jealous of you, Liarhead Liz—"

"Not cool, Kate, not cool."

"I know." She took a deep breath. "I'm sorry. You've been trying to help with April and my mother and I'm lashing out at you. I don't know why."

"Maybe we remind each other of the bad things in our childhoods."

"Maybe you should be studying to be the shrink," Kate said.

"I'll leave that to the smart ones, thanks. But, I am on to something aren't I?"

"Probably. I'd like to call a truce. And as long as you don't hurt Shay, I hope you two do get together."

"I'll accept the truce. And the blessing on my maybe-relationship."

Kate nodded. "Are you coming to the bar for Thanksgiving dinner? They always do quite the spread."

"No, the penitentiary is having dinner for all the inmates and their families. Well, those families who actually visit." *Do not feel sorry for me*, Talia thought. "Last year it was very nice."

✝

When Talia saw the white tablecloths on the tables in the visiting room, she was glad she'd put on a dressy pair of slacks and a blouse. All the visitors were dressed a little nicer than usual, but the inmates still wore their work pants and shirts.

She saw Brian after scanning the room briefly and made her way over to him. The tables were pushed together to create three longer ones. He sat at the table closest to the buffet.

"Tali," he said as he stood and hugged her. "You look great."

"Happy Thanksgiving." She pulled off her coat as she glanced toward the food. "Well, it certainly smells great."

"Yeah, just stay away from the stuffing." He took her coat from her and draped it over the chair beside the one he'd claimed for himself. He leaned close to whisper into her ear, "The cook who made the stuffing cut his finger really bad and bled all over it. They didn't have time to start over so they stuck it in the oven as it was." He gave an exaggerated shudder. "What a shame, since the stuffing is your favorite part of Thanksgiving dinner."

The chatter around them lessened as a chime rang through the room. Over the intercom a voice announced that residents with the last name starting with the letter A through D would go through the buffet line first with their guests.

A low rumble of voices started at the word 'residents.'

100

"I am so glad Mom didn't marry that Zimmerman fellow instead of Dad," Brian said.

When it was their turn to go through the line, Talia followed behind Brian. She spooned spare amounts of green bean casserole, turkey, mashed potatoes with gravy, and corn onto her plate. When she got to the stuffing, she hesitated.

"What's the matter, Tali?" Brian asked. "Still don't know if you believe me or not?"

"Nothing's the matter." She put a decent-sized portion of stuffing onto her plate.

"Remember, it's a crime to waste federal funds so you must eat everything you take."

It was not lost on her that Brian didn't put any stuffing on his plate.

"Don't wait until later to get your dessert, because once the first fight breaks out the food will be taken away."

She wedged a slice of pecan pie between her green bean casserole and corn.

"You have to trust me on this." He gave her a brilliant smile. "Just because we didn't end up with a massive riot last year doesn't mean we won't have one this year."

She hoped he didn't have inside information; that he hadn't manipulated some situation so that it would erupt during the holiday dinner.

To Talia's left, a family of three kids and a woman joined an inmate that Talia recognized from some of the visitation days. She couldn't remember ever seeing the family on visiting days. No, he always met with a younger woman then. She was curious, but it was none of her business.

Brian reached toward her and she thought for a second he was going to take her hand. When he reached past her for the saltshaker he asked, "What?"

"Nothing. I thought maybe you wanted to say grace."

He laughed. "Nah, the Bible-thumping guards aren't here today. Being the good Christians they are, they were given the day off to celebrate with their *families*." He said the word 'families' as if it were a profanity.

Back when their dad was still alive, holiday dinners were a really big deal. He would go overboard on the menu, insisting that every Christmas and Thanksgiving dinner consisted of both ham and turkey, and had a minimum of three different pies for dessert. He always put so much into the meal, and inevitably would get angry at Talia and Brian for something—any little thing—and go into a rage for the rest of the day.

"Do you remember the last Thanksgiving dinner while Dad was alive?" Talia asked Brian.

"Oh, yes, I do," he said.

"I can't remember what it was that pissed Dad off that time."

He turned to face her. "Really? You don't remember?"

She leaned slightly away from him. "No."

"Oh, my God." He slapped his hand on the table and several people looked toward them. "He got angry because you farted during dinner and instead of saying excuse me you giggled."

"No way," she said. That, she would have remembered.

"Yes. He screamed that we were a bunch of animals and didn't deserve his great meal."

She did remember the animals part. She looked at her brother for a long moment. She hated that she never knew when to believe him.

"Oh, maybe it was me who farted. And maybe I said something like, 'There's a kiss for you.' Or not. Maybe it didn't happen that way." He winked at her.

She took a bite of the turkey. It was good. Then she tried the green bean casserole. It was a little salty, but not bad. She sat with her fork hovering above the stuffing.

"Go ahead. Try the stuffing."

She ate a bite of the mashed potatoes.

"Seriously, Tali, aren't you going to try the stuffing? It looks good. Extra moist."

She put some on her fork. She could feel him staring at her. Her fork shook slightly as she forced herself to put the stuffing in her mouth. She took a sip of water.

"Yum," he said.

The couple she'd met the last time she was there sat across the room. She thought she'd catch their eye and smile but they never looked her way. They looked everywhere but toward Talia and Brian. She couldn't help but wonder what Brian had done now. It was probably for the best though, considering they'd gotten away with conspiring to murder the guy's wife.

Talia turned back to her brother. "Did you ever wish you'd be invited up to Mom's for Thanksgiving dinner?" she asked.

Brian knitted his eyebrows together. "What do you mean?"

"Does it hurt your feelings that we were never invited to Mom's in Pennsylvania for any holidays?"

"But I was. Oh, wait. You weren't?"

"What?" Talia asked.

"I never did get that—why Mom invited me up there all the time but didn't want you around her new family."

"You're lying."

He laughed. "Am I? Are you sure?"

She stared at him.

"Look at your face," Brian said. "So drawn and—yeah, we definitely need to work on your poker face."

Talia concentrated on eating the rest of her dinner. She'd cleared her plate of everything but half of the stuffing when Brian jostled her with his elbow.

"What?"

He gestured toward the food line where several men in white aprons were adding food to the serving pans. One of them had a huge bandage on his hand.

"Do you feel a certain bond to that dude refilling the stuffing?"

She set her fork on the side of her plate.

"Eat your dessert, sis."

The expression on his face was so smug and self-satisfied that she had to resist the urge to either slap him, tell him to go to hell, leave early, or all of the above. A question formed in her mind. Psychopath or sociopath? She'd have to ask Kate about the difference between the two.

"Not hungry?" He stuck his fork in the pie and brought it to his own plate. "Suit yourself."

Talia watched as her brother ate his own, then her slice of pie. She drew comfort from the thought that his lying was pathological but hers was learned. He had taught her, and she could unlearn the behavior.

"What?" she asked, aware that she'd tuned out.

"I'm sorry, Tali, is there someplace you'd rather be?"

"No." Her mind drifted to Shay and she felt her face heat up.

"Then quit going someplace else in your mind." He rolled his head, causing his neck to crack several times. "Now, how's the Honda doing?"

"It's good. Still runs great."

His gaze fixed on her, a little too intensely for her comfort. "Glad to hear that."

"Are you still coaching the softball team?" she asked.

"What?"

She wanted to tell him to at least keep his stories straight, but knew it was a moot point. "Nothing. Never mind."

Chapter Eight

Talia ran to answer the ringing phone. She couldn't imagine who would be calling at eight o'clock on a Saturday morning. "Hello." When there was no response, she repeated herself. "Hello?"

She was about to hang up when a small voice asked, "Is this Talia Lisher?"

"Ah, yeah, who's this?" Talia asked.

The woman cleared her throat. "My name is Karen Stephens."

Talia's mouth went dry. After several seconds, she croaked out, "Mrs. Hunter."

"You remember me?" Kate and April's mother asked with surprise.

"Of course. You were one of the few mothers in the neighborhood who was always nice to me."

"How have you been?"

"Ah, I'm fine. You?" She couldn't help but think the small talk was inappropriate.

"I was sorry to hear about your father dying and your brother's problems. I read about that in the newspaper," she added in a rush. "I still read the news from that area."

"Okay." Ask her about leaving her family, Talia pleaded with herself.

"How is your mother, Talia? Did she ever remarry?"

"Yes. And she's fine. I—ah—I don't want to sound judgmental, but shouldn't you be asking me about your own family?" Her question was met with silence on the other end of the phone. "Mrs. Hunter?"

"You're right. I'm sorry. Are Kate and April doing okay? Do you see them still? Did Roger ever remarry?" she blurted out.

"I don't know about your husband. I do see Kate and April around, though."

"The girls are doing okay then?"

How in the hell did she tell this woman that no, they weren't okay, and no, they hadn't adjusted to being abandoned by their mother? "I think you should be asking them these questions."

"I can't," she said as she sniffled. "How could I?"

"Easy. You call them up. You arrange to meet. You tell them you are sorry for disappearing off the face of the earth for all of these years. It really isn't that complicated." Talia stopped her rant. "Oh, my God, I am so sorry, Mrs. Hunter. I have no right—"

"You have every right. You're there with them. I'm not."

"Will you see them? They really want to know that you're—well, alive."

"I don't think I can do that."

"I don't think you can*not* do that." Talia took a deep breath and continued in a softer tone. "You owe it to them."

She could tell Mrs. Hunter was crying.

"I can call them for you. I can arrange for you to see them."

"Will you come with them?"

"If that's what you want," Talia said.

"I do. Maybe you can all three meet me somewhere."

"I can bring them to Roanoke Rapids, if you'd like."

"No. Please. Let's meet somewhere neutral."

Talia took down Mrs. Hunter's phone number and told her she'd call as soon as she could work out a day and time that was okay with Kate and April.

The first thing Talia did when she got off the phone was call Shay. As she told Shay about the conversation, her words rushed out faster and faster.

"Can you tell Kate? I think this should come from you. Then I can make the arrangements," Talia said.

"Okay," Shay said. "You are still coming to the class this afternoon, aren't you?"

Talia smiled. "You aren't nervous about teaching self-defense, are you?"

"I'm not nervous. Well, maybe a little. I've never done anything like this before."

"You're going to be great. Now we both have to get off the phone so we're not late."

"Drive safely. See you soon."

"Yep." Talia hung up and smiled. She couldn't wait for Shay to teach her how to kick some butt.

†

Talia opened the door to the bar and stopped short. She'd never seen it so well-lit nor had she ever seen so many women dressed in sweats—except after a softball practice. She walked in with her gaze glued to Shay. In a pair of shorts and a T-shirt, she looked very nice.

Shay looked up and smiled, causing several women to turn to look where the smile was directed. Talia had never felt so engaged by someone in her entire life. She walked up to the edge of the thick mats that covered the entire dance floor.

"You made it," Shay said.

"I wouldn't have missed it for anything."

"Is this a date or a class?" Brit asked from Talia's left. "Time to teach us your best moves, Shay."

"Okay, everyone." Dee's voice boomed from the microphone in the DJ booth. "Let's get started. I want to start by saying thank you to Shay Eliot for sharing her vast knowledge of self-defense with us. And I want to thank everyone who signed up for the class for coming in and learning how to protect yourselves. Now I'll hand it over to Shay."

"Thanks, Dee. Thanks everyone for coming out—pardon the pun."

Everyone chuckled. Talia smiled.

107

"Come on over and join me on the mats. We're going to start with some warm-up stretching exercises."

"I can see it now," a voice came from the back corner, "wait Mr. Rapist, I haven't stretched yet."

There were a couple of nervous chuckles, but everyone else was silent. Talia looked over her shoulder, trying to see who the voice belonged to.

"I'm pretty sure at least some of you will be doing things today with muscles you don't normally use." Shay looked around. "There's no sense in taking the risk of pulling something now. If you pull something while defending yourself, that will be a lot better than being assaulted—or killed. So for now, we'll be smart and get warmed up."

She led them through some exercises. Talia was surprised how out of shape she was. The way the muscles in the back of her legs and butt were tightening up, she figured she had better do as much stretching as she could.

"I feel empowered already," the voice in the back quipped.

"Tracy, shut up," Dee called out.

"Next week, you can do some stretching before we get started instead. Let's move on," Shay said.

Shay had all the women line up on the edge of the mat, facing her. "When it's all said and done, the best defense is avoidance. Be aware of and avoid potentially dangerous situations."

"In other words, no screwing on the Colonial Parkway," Tracy said.

"Out!" Dee yelled as she rushed toward Tracy. "Get out of this bar and do not come back!"

"Bunch of stupid bitches," Tracy called back over her shoulder as she left.

"So," Shay said, her voice a little flatter. "Where were we?"

"Avoidance," Talia said. She hated that anyone would try to make light of how every other person in the room felt. She looked around. Everyone in there wanted to feel safer.

Shay smiled at her, then turned to the rest of the women. "So, you find yourself in a potentially dangerous situation. If you can— run. If prevention and running away are out of the question or aren't an option, your next step is to get loud and push back," Shay said. "As soon as you know escape isn't an option, shout as loud as you can, 'BACK OFF!'"

Talia and several others jumped.

"See there, surprised you, didn't I?" Shay asked. "When you shout like that, you not only draw attention to yourself and possibly alert someone who can help, you also surprise your attacker. Give a shove when you shout." She looked around. "Ginny, come at me like you're my assailant."

Ginny walked toward Shay, squaring her shoulders and acting cocky. "Hey little girl, let me show you som'fin'," she joked. She reached for Shay.

"Back off!" Shay yelled as she shoved Ginny hard, making her almost lose her balance. "See, I'm not such an easy target, am I?" She motioned toward Ginny.

Ginny started toward Shay again, and again Shay yelled and shoved. Ginny would have fallen if two women hadn't kept her from tripping backward.

"For the record, I'm letting you do that to me," Ginny quipped.

"Of course you are, pal," Shay said. "If she was to keep coming at me after I yelled and shoved, it would be the time to commit myself one hundred percent to causing injury to my attacker. There is no room to be indecisive or tentative. Go for the eyes, nose, neck, groin, knees, or shins." She looked at all the women as she spoke. "Let's pair up and take turns practicing being loud and shoving. But remember it's just an exercise. Don't try to land your partner on their butts, okay? There will be plenty of that in future classes."

There was a slight rise in the noise level as the women murmured while pairing up. Ginny took Talia by the arm and led her a few feet into the center of the mat. "Come on, show me what you got," she said.

Suddenly the noise level went through the roof. Eleven pairs of women took turns shouting and shoving. Talia tried to concentrate on what she was doing, but was so engrossed in the sounds of women being empowered that she got a little distracted and almost fell when Ginny shoved her.

"Very good everyone," Shay called out over the roar. "Now let's talk about the most effective places to hit your attacker because as I said, you must commit to hurting your attacker at this point."

Talia was fired up. Yes, she could hurt someone if they were trying to hurt her or someone she loved.

"To cause the most damage, go for the eyes, nose, neck, knees, shins, and groin. Hit them to hurt them, to incapacitate them, then get the hell out of there." She looked around at all the women. "So, for the eyes—poke, gouge, or scratch. For the nose— use the heel of your palm to strike up under the nose."

"Dee, your turn."

Dee approached her. "Hurt me and you're fired."

Shay laughed. "Just stand right here in front of me. I won't even make contact."

Dee moved closer.

Shay demonstrated the hand position for hitting with the heel of her palm in an upward motion. "Just like that. For a blow to the neck, hold your hand like this," she said as she held up her hand with fingers extended, and showed them a fake chop motion to Dee's neck. "Or you can force your elbow into their throat."

Dee took a step back.

"Damn, Dee, have some trust in me."

Everyone laughed.

"For groin, knees and shins, you kick, punch, elbow, whatever you can and do it hard."

"Very hard," someone added.

"Yes, very hard," Shay agreed. "Next week, we'll go over different moves to defend against common holds. Okay, ready to stretch some more?"

There were a few groans, but everyone fell right in with the stretches Shay was demonstrating.

"Thank you all for coming out. Thank you for wanting to learn to protect yourselves. Please remember that by keeping your

Renee MacKenzie

bodies in good shape you are helping to protect yourselves as well. Good night."

The next day, Shay watched Kate's expression carefully as Talia told her about the conversation she'd had with the woman who was probably her mother. She and Talia had already discussed the possibility that Karen Stephens wasn't really Karen Hunter and was just playing some sick game with them. Talia had thought the voice sounded like her, but couldn't be sure after all these years.

"If this isn't her, and we drag April out there, it could devastate her," Shay said, wanting to be sure they thought it out completely.

"If it *is* her, it could devastate April." Kate massaged her temples. "I don't know what to do. If I don't say anything to April and meet her and it is Mom...what if she says to not come back and I cause April to miss her only chance to see her?"

"Ultimately it's your decision, Kate. But I really think excluding April would be a huge mistake. I know she's fragile, but she has a right to decide for herself if she wants to go see if it is your mother," Talia said.

"She's right," Shay said. She was so impressed with how Talia had handled the situation so far. Even when Kate's initial reaction was that Talia might be lying about the whole thing, Talia shrugged it off.

"I'll call April tonight and see what she wants to do. Can you arrange a time and place?" Kate asked Talia.

"Just give me the word."

Shay saw Kate out and then rejoined Talia in the living room where she was on the sofa petting Poke.

"He really likes you," Shay said.

"He's a sweetie." Talia looked at Shay with pursed lips.

"What are you thinking?"

"I hope this thing works out with the Hunters. It sure would be nice to have some good closure what with everything else still open, you know?"

Yes, Shay knew. She studied Talia and a warmth spread through her. The young woman was really growing on her. Shay had made a point to keep things uncomplicated with her, especially given the fact that Talia had been stalking her at one time. However, she now felt that they'd moved well beyond that in their friendship.

"I should get going. Brian's phone time was switched to tonight since Thursday was Thanksgiving." Talia moaned as she stood and stretched. "Damn, I feel like I've had my ass whipped."

"You did." Shay laughed. "You're a good sister. And you're being a good friend to Kate as well. I forgot to ask you how Thanksgiving dinner went with your brother."

"It was pretty nice. The penitentiary did a good job with the dinner. Your holiday at your parents' went well?"

"Yeah, it was good."

Talia started for the door.

Shay met her there and before Talia could open the door, Shay turned her around and gave her a light kiss on the lips. "Drive safely."

Talia smiled. "I will."

Shay followed her out to her car and stood in the driveway watching the Honda move down the road. She shook off the queasiness that threatened her when the back of Talia's car brought back the memory of a different silver Honda, one jammed into the brush on the side of the parkway in one of the crime scene photos. She forced the image out of her head.

When Talia turned at the intersection and drove out of sight, Shay went inside. She sat on the edge of the sofa and reflected on the vulnerability she saw in Talia during the class. It made her feel as if she wanted to teach her everything she knew about staying safe and to always be there to protect her.

†

"Hey, thanks for meeting me," Lana said as Shay approached her in front of the Chinese restaurant for lunch. Lana had suggested meeting for lunch to help keep her occupied while Kate went to meet the woman who claimed to be her mother.

"So, I'm finally going to get you to try some Chinese food, huh?"

"I'm not making any promises," Lana said.

Shay looked her up and down. "You've been painting."

"Yeah. Sorry, I lost track of time and didn't get a chance to shower and change."

When the waitress brought menus, they ordered sodas then Shay leaned across the table to point out a few items she thought Lana might like.

"I'd better go with the vegetable fried rice," Lana said.

"That's very good here. I think I'll start with an eggroll and also have the fried rice," Shay said.

Lana checked her watch. "Do you think they're in Emporia yet?"

Shay glanced toward the clock on the wall behind the hostess stand. "Probably not quite there."

Their drinks arrived and they ordered their lunch. "I guess Kate was nervous?"

"That's an understatement." Lana took a sip of her soda. "She hardly slept at all last night."

"I hope she's not disappointed."

"Mrs. Hunter will show up, won't she?" Lana asked.

Shay shrugged. "Nothing people do or don't do surprises me anymore."

Lana leaned forward. "So, tell me about you and Talia."

"What about me and Talia?" Shay asked.

"Come on. The looks between you two are too obvious to deny."

Shay could feel the heat spreading up her neck, lingering at her cheeks.

"Well, for the record, I really like Talia, and I think you two would be great together," Lana asserted.

Shay had a fleeting thought that maybe Lana was just glad Shay was looking at someone other than her girlfriend. Then she felt a surge of guilt because Lana had never been anything but a good friend and had never said or done anything that would suggest that she harbored that kind of thought.

"So?" Lana prompted.

Shay smiled. "Thank you for being a good friend. I do care a lot for Talia, and it means so much that you acknowledge that and, well, give us your support."

A group of four guys came in, talking loudly.

"Lana?" Shay and Lana both turned to look at one of the young men.

"Benji?" Lana stood up and gave him a hug.

Shay heard him mumble, "It's Ben now."

"Ben." Lana stepped back and gave him an appraising look. "You're all grown up."

Ben smiled. "Yes, I am." He seemed to grow shy. "I've missed you, Lana."

"I've missed you too." She turned to Shay. "Shay, this is Benj—I mean Ben Davis."

Shay stood and extended her hand. "Shay Eliot. It's nice to meet you."

"Um, Ben is Richie's brother," Lana said.

"Oh." Shay didn't know what else to say. An image of Lana's boyfriend, Richie Davis, bloodied and barely alive, rushed at her. She was at the scene of the assault on him. It was the last time she would see Richie alive; he died from the massive blunt force trauma shortly after.

"Did you know my brother?" Ben asked Shay.

"Not exactly." She held his gaze and hoped he wouldn't want an explanation.

He cocked his head but brought his attention back to Lana. "Where've you been? What are you up to?"

Shay could tell the wheels were spinning as Lana struggled to find the words.

"I see you're still painting, that's good," Ben said as he nodded toward her paint-splattered jeans.

Lana looked down at her Levi's. "Yeah, I'm still painting."

"Dude, you eating or what?" one of the other guys called out to Ben.

"Yeah, I'm eating." He turned back to Lana. "It was great to see you. Can I get your number? You know, so we can talk about Richie sometime?"

"I, ah—" She looked down as she stammered.

"Sorry, I didn't mean to put you on the spot. I better get over to my buddies." He gave a half-hearted smile and walked away.

"Okay, that was awkward," Lana muttered as she sat back down.

Shay noticed the color leaving Lana's face. "Are you okay?"

"I haven't seen him since Richie's funeral," she whispered.

"I'm sorry." Shay sat back down.

"He was a bit like a little brother to me. Maybe I shouldn't have fallen off the face of the earth like that."

"You were grieving."

"*He* was grieving." Lana glanced toward Ben. "He lost the most important person in his life and I wasn't around to help him make sense of it."

"You had your own issues to deal with." Shay crossed her arms over her chest. "Did you want to give him your number?"

Lana looked away. "Yeah. I do miss him."

"Then maybe you should."

"That wouldn't be fair to Kate." She sat back as the waitress placed their lunches on the table. "Sometimes I get the feeling she's halfway waiting for me to leave her for a man."

"And?"

"And what?"

"Are you?" Shay asked.

"You really have to ask?"

Shay smiled. "I see how you look at Kate. But I can also understand her insecurities. No one wants to think they have competition from players on both teams."

"This isn't a game."

"Oh, I know that. Just make sure she knows that you don't think it is."

Ben and the other guys left. He gave them a nod of his head and disappeared with his buddies.

The waitress came by to refill their drinks. "Can we have the check, please?"

"Oh," she said. "The young man who just left paid your bill."

They both looked toward the door.

"He asked me to give you this." The waitress gave Lana a napkin with a phone number scrawled on it.

After the waitress left, Lana moved as if to crumple it up.

"You should keep it. One day you might need to talk to someone who actually knew Richie."

"But—"

"I'm just saying put it away until you know for sure that you don't want or need to call and talk to Ben."

"I'm not going to hide anything from Kate."

"I didn't suggest that you do. The next conversation should be between you and Kate," Shay said.

✝

Talia had a death grip on the steering wheel. She glanced over at Kate, then in the rearview mirror at April and her heart started pounding. She prayed Mrs. Hunter would show up in Emporia as planned.

She wished for the hundredth time that Shay could have come with them, but Mrs. Hunter had insisted it only be Kate, April, and Talia.

The thought of Shay kissing her goodbye two days earlier made Talia smile. It had been just a light kiss, but was so sweet, and Talia had smiled the whole way home. Later, on the phone, Brian kept asking her what her deal was, accusing her of sounding unusually happy. Of course she told him she didn't know what he meant.

"Where are we meeting her?" Kate asked.

"A gas station by the interstate. There's a little food place where we can get burgers and sit down to talk." Talia watched April in the rearview mirror as she spoke. April's blank look never changed

"You okay back there?" Kate asked.

"Fine."

Talia wondered if April was wishing she'd brought Joseph, or if she was glad for the break. Joey had taken the day off from work so April could have some 'girl time.' Talia wasn't sure if April had even told her husband what they were doing that day.

The first thing Talia noticed as she turned into the parking lot at the gas station was that most of the vehicles were pickup trucks. The second thing she noticed was that there were only men around. No women, most notably, no Mrs. Hunter.

Talia parked her Honda around the side of the building. They waited.

"How long should we give her?" Kate asked.

"I have to pee," was the only response April gave.

"Me too. I'll go with you," Talia said. "You want to come with us, Kate?"

"Yeah, I'll go too." Kate looked around. "We should probably lock up the car."

The restrooms were around the back, required a key attached to a large wooden spoon, and appeared not to have been cleaned in months.

After taking turns and returning the key to the cashier, the three headed back to the car. Kate was in the lead and as she rounded the building she came to an abrupt halt. April plowed into the back of her and was in midprotest when Talia saw Mrs. Hunter standing beside a white pickup with Winston's Plumbing stenciled on the side and a nervous-looking man watching from inside the cab. She recognized Winston right away and gave him a weak smile. He nodded.

"Hi," Kate stammered.

Talia watched a string of expressions pass across April's face. When April wobbled, Talia put her hand on her elbow.

"Hi girls," Mrs. Hunter said, almost too cheerily.

"Hello," Talia said. She was amazed at how much Mrs. Hunter looked exactly the same as she did fifteen years earlier. A few lines were etched around her mouth and eyes, and a line of gray was visible along her part where her hair had started to grow out of its dye job, but otherwise, she'd barely changed.

"Kate thought they fished your body from the York River," April blurted. "But I knew it wasn't you. I've always known you were still alive."

Mrs. Hunter looked confused, like she was trying to decide if that warranted a thank-you or an I'm sorry. "Do you girls want to go next door for a burger? My treat," Mrs. Hunter said.

Kate glanced at the others. "Okay."

"Should I hang out here?" Talia asked.

"No, please. Come on with us." There was an edge of desperation to Mrs. Hunter's voice.

The four women sat around a table after placing their order at a counter. When their number was called, Talia went to pick up the tray of food.

"So, Kate, you have a son?"

Everyone stared at Mrs. Hunter.

"When Talia and the private investigator talked to Winston—"

"Private investigator?" April asked.

"PI Eliot," Talia answered, really liking the sound of that.

April still looked confused, but Kate smiled at Talia.

"April has a son, Mom," Kate said, hesitating slightly at the word 'mom.'

"Yeah, Mom," April said. "I have a son with my ex-drug dealer husband. I was going to marry my other boyfriend, Boyd, but he was murdered..." she glared at Kate as she spoke.

Talia choked on a sip of her soda.

"There, now you're all caught up on current events. Oh— except the part where Dad almost killed Cousin Bobby when he caught him fingering me when I was nine." April sat back and crossed her arms over her chest.

Talia glanced around. Every person in the room was gawking at them. Mrs. Hunter had almost no color to her face.

"I...ah...I don't know what to say..." Mrs. Hunter swallowed hard. "So...well, then. Ah—Kate, tell me about your—your lover," she said.

Kate sat up straighter. "Her name is Lana. We've been together for about three years now." She took a quick bite of her burger.

Mrs. Hunter sat stock-still for several moments before she smiled.

Talia wondered if her friends' mother's responses seemed so muted because she was on some kind of medication.

Mrs. Hunter cleared her throat. "You girls are so beautiful." She pushed her plate away from her. "Let me start by saying that I am truly sorry for leaving you and I never stopped loving either of you."

Talia looked from Kate to April and back. Tears filled Kate's eyes as she kept them glued to her mom. April stared down into her lap.

"Why did you leave?" Kate asked, her voice a whisper.

"I was so overwhelmed. And it scared me." She twisted her napkin as she spoke. "I know now that I had postpartum depression, but at the time I just thought I was crazy."

Kate and Talia both looked briefly at April. Talia was pretty sure it was noticed by Mrs. Hunter.

"I was so sad all the time," Mrs. Hunter continued. "And I worried about hurting you both. I-I-"

"You what, Mom?" Kate encouraged her.

"I had thoughts of hurting you girls. It was as if I couldn't control myself so I left so I wouldn't hurt you. Or worse. Every time there is a news story about a mother drowning or strangling her children, I think that could have been me. That would have been me had I stayed."

They all turned toward April when she gasped. After several moments, she said, "I quit bathing Joseph. I kept thinking about drowning him and not accidentally."

Kate's mouth opened, but nothing came out. She paled.

Talia was shocked by the enormity of what April had admitted and how hard that must have been for her.

"There are things you can do for that," Kate finally said. "Therapy is working wonders on PPD." She looked back and forth between her mom and sister and then said to her mom, "I'm studying psychology in college. I want to be a therapist when I'm done."

"I wish I had known what was happening to me. I wish I had stayed and tried to fix it, but I was scared to death. Your dad was gone for work a lot and every time he left I thought, this will be the time I snap."

April got up and left the restaurant without another word.

"Should I go after her?" Kate asked no one in particular.

"How about I go check on her? You stay here and catch up more with your mother." Talia stood as she spoke.

April had stopped right outside of the building. Talia leaned with her back against the restaurant's brick wall.

"I don't think I can forgive her for leaving," April said without looking at Talia.

"No one is saying you have to." Talia pivoted so her shoulder was pressed against the brick and she was facing April. "But this is your chance...your chance to say whatever you want to your mom, or your chance to say nothing at all. Don't you want to go in and make the most of this opportunity?"

April pushed off from the wall and walked so fast back into the restaurant that Talia had to run to catch up.

Kate and Mrs. Hunter watched as Talia and April sat back down.

"April," Mrs. Hunter's voice was shaky at first, then steadied. "Please get some help. If not in a group setting then at least with a qualified therapist."

April nodded but didn't look up.

"And Kate, good luck with school. I know you'll do great."

"You're saying goodbye, aren't you, Mom?" Kate asked.

"I'm so sorry. This has been great. But I'm no more prepared now to be a mother than I was when I left you girls. I look at you and I feel panicked all over again."

"You can't hurt us now. Not physically anyway," Kate said.

"I don't want to go back to that dark place," Mrs. Hunter whispered, her voice ragged. "And if I try to be your mother again, I'm afraid that's exactly where I'll end up."

Kate fished around in her purse. She pulled out paper and a pen and wrote down her number. "If you ever want to get together again. Or to just talk. Call me anytime."

Karen swiped at a tear. "Thank you."

"I'm not giving you my number. You were a coward then and you're a coward now," April said. "I'll get the help I need and in the end I'll be a great mother. Not like you." She stood. "I'll be waiting at the car. Don't come out until we're ready to leave." She directed the last statement at Talia.

"Maybe in time," Talia muttered to Karen and Kate.

Karen gave her a sad smile. "You have been so sweet, Talia. I admire the young woman you've turned into."

"Thanks," Talia said.

Kate and her mom embraced, hugging for a long time. Talia walked out and went toward the car where April was waiting. Her heart broke for April, but she was glad that Kate seemed to be doing well with it all.

They drove back to Norfolk without talking.

Chapter Nine

Shay could tell Talia was surprised, in a very good way, when she answered the door and Shay was standing there. She invited Shay in, and then disappeared long enough to change out of her work garb.

"Can I take you out to dinner?" Shay asked.

"Well, yes, you may."

Shay looked her over, pleased at the sight of Talia in dark gray slacks and a pale gray sweater. In her black slacks and a white button-down, Shay couldn't help but think they looked really good together.

They stopped in the parking lot and Shay asked, "Which car would you like to take?"

"We can take mine." Talia held out the keys. "But would you mind driving?"

"Not at all," Shay said as Talia dropped the keys into her palm.

At the restaurant, Talia ordered a Greek salad, minus the onions, and Shay ordered the cheeseburger boat. As soon as their food came out Shay wondered, based on the way she was eyeing her french fries, if Talia regretted her food choice.

"Would you like a french fry?" Shay asked.

"I thought you'd never ask." Talia grabbed one and shoved it into her mouth.

Shay laughed. "They are very good."

"I'm looking forward to Saturday's class. I hated missing last week, but by the time we got back from seeing Mrs. Hunter in Emporia I was exhausted," Talia said.

"I'm looking forward to Saturday as well. And I totally understand you missing it last week. Besides, I'm more than willing to give you private lessons anytime you want them."

Talia smiled. "I may take you up on that."

As they were leaving, Shay asked if she'd been on the Colonial Parkway lately.

"No. How about you?"

"I've never been on the parkway. In high school we had fieldtrips to Yorktown, Williamsburg, and Jamestown. But I don't recall being on the parkway." She shrugged. "Once I left Richmond years ago, I never really came over to this side of the tunnel. Until I met you." For Shay, the Hampton Roads Bridge-Tunnel, with its trestles and man-made islands in addition to the bridges and tunnels, definitively separated Shay's world from Talia's.

"I only go to the other side of the tunnel for the bar."

"And to watch me," Shay said with a smile and a wink.

"Yes, and to watch you." As they approached Talia's car, she asked, "Do you want me to show you where they found the bodies?"

"Would you?"

"Of course. If you will protect me."

"Of course. And I hope you don't go out there alone anymore."

Talia told her where to turn and in no time they were on the parkway. The sun was just starting to set.

"It's beautiful out here."

"Yeah, and forever ruined for a lot of people," Talia said. "Just up there on the right..." she started to say when the squealing of tires interrupted her.

The dark blue van, with tires squealing, made a U-turn and came up behind them.

"Hang on," Shay said.

She took the lane to go into the overlook and slammed on the brakes. The van pulled off too but had to swerve to the left to keep from hitting them. Then it stopped.

Before Shay could think about what she was doing, she was out of the car and dragging a man out of the van. He swung at her. She ducked, then with a quick uppercut punched him in the stomach. While he was struggling to breathe, she took a few steps to the back of the van and checked the tag. It matched the one from that night at the bar. It had the same dented ladder on the back as well. She coughed when the diesel exhaust threatened to choke her.

She glanced back to where he was standing and found that he was still doubled over.

"Why are you following this woman, Jeffrey?" Shay asked.

"How the hell do you know my name?" he asked, catching his breath.

"Why are you following her?" she yelled and nodded toward Talia.

"That's Brian's car and something in there belongs to me." He started to straighten. "That bitch needs to give me a few minutes with the car and I'll leave her alone."

She kicked his legs out from under him. "Call her that again and you'll get it in the groin next. You want that?"

"No," he whined, clawing at the ground on his hands and knees.

"You stay the hell away from her, you hear me?"

"I want my shit back and I will get it, one way or another."

Shay looked at Talia and she shrugged.

"What's in there that belongs to you?" Shay asked.

"Fuck you, bitch." He started to get up.

Shay was about to kick him again when Talia said, "Hey."

Talia turned to look over her shoulder, and Shay followed her gaze. A park ranger's car pulled up. Shay let Jeffrey get to his feet.

The ranger rolled down his window and stared at them. "Is everything all right here?"

Shay couldn't help but think about the theory that the murders were committed by a park ranger. She wondered how many people would never trust another one of them again.

"Yes, sir, everything here is great," Talia said.

Shay took a step back. "Yep, all is good here."

"It's getting late. You all move along now. I don't want to see you pulled off again tonight. Understood?"

"Yes sir," Shay and Talia said in unison. They slowly got in the car and waited until Jeffrey pulled out. Shay noted the dark, diesel exhaust as the van pulled away. She turned in the opposite direction and the ranger pulled out behind them. Shay was careful to stay right at the speed limit. She was pretty sure if the ranger tried to stop her she wouldn't pull over, at least not until they got off the parkway and into a more populated area. She hated this feeling of fear and distrust. A few minutes later they got off the parkway and the ranger kept going.

Shay checked the rearview mirror before every turn. When she was confident the van wasn't anywhere around them, she pulled into the parking lot of Talia's apartment complex and they went inside without a word.

Once inside Talia's apartment, it really hit Shay. She had put them both at risk by asking Talia to go to the parkway, and especially by getting out of the car to confront Jeffrey Gardner. What if he'd had a gun? He could have killed them both.

Talia grabbed two beers out of the fridge, then put them back and pulled out two sodas.

"Talia, that was a really dumb move on my part. I am so sorry. That could have turned ugly very fast."

"It's okay. It is. I just want to figure this out because I want to know what he thinks I have of his."

Shay nodded. "What's in your car that he would want?"

"I have cleaned that car a million times and as far as I know there is nothing in there."

"Do you have anything else of your brother's?"

"Not really. Some clothes in the closet and his albums. It's got to be in his car, like Jeffrey said."

"We should do a thorough search inside it, but it'll be hard to see much at night though."

"Like I said, I've cleaned that car so many times, inside and out, and if there is anything in there it has to be well hidden."

"Grab a flashlight and let me take a quick look."

Talia got one from the kitchen and followed her out. They looked all through the car and found nothing except for a few pot seeds that they immediately flushed down the toilet when they went back inside.

They went through Brian's things in the closet and found nothing that they felt Jeffrey would be after. Talia picked through pockets and Shay felt around the liners of his jackets and coats, and looked in his shoes.

They pulled every album out of its sleeve and checked the jackets. There was nothing.

Talia went to the La-Z-Boy chair. "My mom left this behind. Maybe Brian hid something in here before he left." She ran her fingers along the cushions.

Shay could tell Talia was frustrated and frantic. She watched as Talia got a knife out of the kitchen and sliced open the backing material on the chair.

"Can you grab the flashlight?" Talia asked her. "I put it back in the kitchen."

Shay shined the light into the back of the chair. They didn't see anything. Talia reached under the chair with the knife and sliced the bottom lining. She shoved her hand in and a spring jammed her finger, making her cry out. When she straightened up, she held the knife firm in her grip, as if preparing to hack open the cushions.

Shay grabbed her by her arm. "Put the knife down, Talia. There's nothing in this chair."

"But there has to be. Where else could it be? Oh." She stopped and looked toward the door. "The seats. Maybe it's hidden in the car's seats."

"You aren't taking a knife to the car," Shay said. "Why don't you call your brother and ask him what's going on?"

"He'll just lie. He'll think he's doing me a favor and lie about it." She started crying.

"Give me the knife," Shay said, her voice gentle.

"I don't want to keep looking over my shoulder. Everyone has been so on edge since the murders. I can't take this fear of Jeffrey on top of the stress of the other stuff going on." She let Shay take the knife out of her hand.

When she started to shake Shay hugged her. "I know, I know," Shay whispered.

All Shay wanted to do was to make Talia feel better. She forced the thought of how wonderful Talia felt from her mind. This was not the time or the place to have those kinds of thoughts about her.

Talia sobbed and Shay held her tighter. "It's okay, we'll figure this out."

"Where else could it be?"

Shay stepped away from the embrace. "Maybe we should take a closer look at your car." She glanced at the knife she'd set on the coffee table. "But let's do it gently."

"What do you have in mind?" Talia asked.

"I have a friend who's really good with this sort of thing. Let me see about enlisting her help. Why don't you pack a bag and stay at my house tonight?"

Talia followed Shay to her house, where she again parked in the backyard.

✝

The next morning Talia called in sick even though she knew Dr. Bennett frowned on her taking Fridays off. He always thought it was just to make a long weekend. Shay drove Talia's car to her friend's garage. Mindy was a mechanic and the police department often used her when they needed help finding evidence in cars.

Talia would have liked the short, stocky woman in the coveralls even if she hadn't overheard her whisper to Shay, "Your girlfriend is a real cutie."

When Shay's response was a blush and no correction of Mindy's word choice, Talia felt a flutter in her belly. That was her first sign since their brief kiss that maybe there was hope in them transcending friendship one day after all.

Wearing latex gloves, Mindy searched the trunk. She removed parts of the flooring, searched around the spare tire, and pulled out the jack to examine it. She was gentle, just like Shay promised. An hour later, the mechanic moved to the glove box with a screw driver. "Bingo," she called out only moments later.

As she removed the false back to the glove box, Talia and Shay leaned closer to see what was there. "Whoa," Mindy said.

They all stared at a bundle of cash, a leather wallet-like holder, and a revolver.

"Holy crap," Shay said. "That's for a badge." She motioned toward the leather item.

Talia closed her eyes tight. "Oh Brian, what have you done?"

Mindy splayed the stash across the passenger seat. "What now?"

"We have to turn it in." Shay looked at Talia as she spoke.

"Yes we do," Talia agreed.

No one moved.

"They'll keep your car as evidence," Mindy said.

"Forever?" Talia asked.

"Not forever," Shay said. "Although it might feel like it, but we'll get you hooked up with something in the meantime."

Shay called Parker to come make the first report. Then she called a few people she knew who had spare vehicles.

Two hours later, after talking to Officer Parker and a detective, Talia drove home in Dee's Mazda pickup, bumper stickers announcing to the world that she loved rock and roll, desired world peace, and wanted to save the whales.

†

Talia spent the next morning cleaning her apartment. She was wearing a hooded sweatshirt and jeans when she heard a knock on her door. She looked through the peephole and saw two people, a man and a woman, each in a dark suit. She knew it wasn't someone selling vacuum cleaners on this Saturday morning, not dressed like that. She kept the door's security chain engaged and opened it two inches.

"Talia Lisher?"

"Yes," she croaked out.

"I am FBI Special Agent Angela Gish and this is Agent Nathan Jackson. May we come in, please?" The female agent flashed her badge quickly and the male held his up for several moments.

Talia closed the door to disengage the door chain. She glanced behind her as panic swept through her. She then remembered she hadn't had any drugs in her apartment for some time and they probably didn't give a crap about that anyway.

She opened the door and stepped aside as the agents came in. "Are you alone?" Agent Jackson asked, his voice low.

Talia grew scared at the way his hand rested on his gun as he looked around.

"Yes, I'm alone."

"Sit down," he said.

She did as she was told and he started methodically going through her rooms. The female agent waited with her.

"Clear," he said as he rejoined them.

"As I said before, I'm Agent Gish and this is Agent Jackson." The woman nodded toward the other agent.

"When's the last time you saw Brian Lisher?" Agent Jackson asked.

"I went to visit him the other—" she couldn't remember when that had been "—the other day."

"At the prison?" Jackson asked.

"Of course at the prison. Where else would I have—" She stopped short. "Oh, my God, where's my brother?"

"You don't know?" Gish asked.

"He's not in Brookeville at the prison, is he?" She started to shake.

"No, he is not. Do you know where he is?" Jackson asked.

"No."

"Has he been in touch with you since he left the facility?"

"Of course not." She hugged her arms to herself. "I'm going to get a soda, if that's okay," Talia said.

The agents exchanged glances and Agent Jackson nodded. When Talia came out of the kitchen she popped the top of her Coke and took a long swallow as tears coursed down her face.

"We need to ask you a couple more questions," Jackson said, almost apologetically.

"Okay," Talia sputtered.

"Do you know where the money and gun came from?"

"No."

"The car was originally your brother's?"

"Yes. Maybe Brian didn't know it was there. He wanted me to have something nice since he was leaving me all alone. Maybe he—"

"Miss Lisher, please," Agent Gish said as she leaned slightly forward in her chair. "Just let us ask you a few more questions, okay?"

Talia pulled her legs up onto the La-Z-Boy and wrapped her arms around them. She wished Shay was with her because she would feel so much safer if she were there. Then she thought, what if Shay was going to distance herself now? She couldn't really blame her if she did, not with all the drama Talia had brought into her life since she started stalking her.

"Miss Lisher, did you hear the question?" Jackson asked.

"No. Sorry."

"How do you know Jeffrey Gardner?"

She didn't know how to answer. If she told the truth, would she get Shay in trouble? If she lied... well then she would lose Shay for sure. "I don't actually know him. I'd never even seen him before he started following me. Then when—when I did talk to him he said my brother had something that belonged to him."

Agent Gish maintained eye contact with Talia for several moments. "You never spoke to Jeffrey before the time you and Shay Eliot confronted him on the parkway about following you?"

Talia instinctively knew she was telling her that Shay had told them everything already, and that she was free to talk. She opened up to them then, reliving every moment of every encounter she'd had with Jeffrey Gardner.

"Do you have any idea where your brother might be?"

She racked her brain. There was no place in particular she could think of. "No, not really."

"Is there somewhere you would rather stay for a while?" Gish asked her.

Talia rocked back and forth. "I don't know. I don't know what to do."

"Talia, are you afraid of your brother?" Jackson asked.

She couldn't answer. All she could think of was how he didn't protect her from Timmy Hall that day all those years ago when she changed her story about riding his bicycle.

"We'll keep your apartment under surveillance in case your brother comes here looking for you," Jackson said. "Also, with your permission, we would like to put a tracer on your phone."

"Do you need to call someone now? Maybe Shay Eliot?" Agent Gish asked.

Talia thought about Shay and wished she was here with her. She didn't want to call Shay, not until after she taught her self-defense class that afternoon, the class Talia would now be missing for the second week in a row.

Chapter Ten

Talia looked around at all the equipment on her kitchen counter. She didn't even know how most of it worked. Electronic boxes covered the counter and wires stretched across the floor, all to trace and record her incoming calls. The agents and technicians had promised they would not record calls Talia made to other people, but Talia wasn't sure she believed that.

She always had at least two officers and/or agents inside the apartment with her and the technician. There was another person watching her Honda from the far corner of the parking lot.

Talia wondered if Maybe Lesbian had figured out something odd was going on. She hadn't seen her in a while, but then again Talia wasn't following her usual routine at the moment either.

Agent Jackson gestured toward the sofa when he addressed Talia. She sat on the edge, too keyed up to sit back.

"Does the name Robert Sanford mean anything to you?"

Talia looked from Agent Jackson to Agent Gish and shook her head.

Agent Jackson showed Talia a picture. "This is Robert Sanford."

"Oh, yeah. I met him when I was visiting Brian. He was in the room next to Brian's, I believe." She thought about the discomfort he showed when Brian watched him, and then how he and his sister-in-law wouldn't look over in Talia and Brian's direction at Thanksgiving dinner. "Why?"

"His statement to authorities would indicate you are in danger from Jeffrey Gardner."

"That's nothing new, right?"

"It is in that Jeffrey has said things to your brother indicating that. We think those threats might be behind the timing of Brian's disappearance."

"How *did* he do that?" Talia asked. She still couldn't believe he had just walked right out of a federal penitentiary.

"We are still investigating. It seems he may have gotten a hold of some forged release papers."

"But you think he left to protect me from Jeffrey?" That should make her feel a little better about it, right?

"We cannot assume anything with someone like Brian Lisher."

The way Agent Jackson said that made Talia's skin crawl. "What exactly did Jeffrey say to Brian about me?"

The agents exchanged glances then Agent Gish spoke. "That he would hurt you if he didn't get what he wanted."

"The gun and the money?"

"We believe so."

"Where does Robert Sanford fit into this?"

"He overheard the threat."

"And you believe someone who would kill his own wife for the insurance money?" Talia asked.

"What?" Agent Gish looked at Talia. "He's in for tax fraud. His wife is alive and well and we hear visits him every week."

"Oh." Talia swallowed the disappointment that her brother lied about that to her. Once upon a time they lied to everyone else, not each other. *Except me, when it came to the day Dad died.*

†

Talia leaned against the kitchen counter as she talked to Shay on the phone.

"You sure you want to go in to work?" Shay asked.

"I need to because I can't continue to hide. Besides, Agent Gish said they'd have someone on me around the clock," Talia said.

"Stay vigilant."

"I will." After disconnecting, she clutched the phone to her chest until she caught Agent Gish watching her with a knowing smile. She smiled back, then headed out the door.

Talia pretended not to notice the unmarked car parked two buildings down. She felt compelled to do the speed limit since law enforcement officers were following her. She wondered if they were FBI or local cops and how they felt being stuck keeping an eye on her.

She made it to work with plenty of time to spare. Since Dr. Bennett hadn't entrusted her with keys to the office, she had to wait until someone else arrived to go in. The receptionist, Sally, looked at Talia, then at the only other car in the parking lot. Talia was sure that even someone whose world was as narrow as Sally's could figure out the other car had two cops in it and why they were there.

Talia gave Sally time to get in and get settled. Maybe they wouldn't have to fake small talk niceties before the first patient arrived.

Dr. Bennett came in and spoke in low tones with Sally, then asked Talia to join them in his office. "I see we have company in the parking lot," Dr. Bennett said.

"Yeah. Sorry about that. It's just a precaution, they really don't expect—"

"Talia, I have to ask you to leave and don't come back. When I gave you the job here I was trying to show you my faith in your ability to overcome your family's...issues."

Talia started to zone out but forced herself to listen. When she thought back on this and hated him for his words, she wanted to do so accurately. She stared at a stone model on the dentist's desk recognizing it as one she'd poured. She'd know that crooked lateral incisor anywhere after working on the patient for months.

"But obviously your family problems are going to follow you. I can't have you here and have escaped criminals coming around

Renee MacKenzie

embezzler is a big deal, but I do, and our patients do as well. So
please, gather your things and leave. Sally will see to it that your
final paycheck is mailed to you."

"*My* people? Seriously?" She stopped herself from telling him
to cram his condescending attitude up his ass. It crossed her mind
to snatch the stone model off his desk and leave with it. She'd
gotten really good at pouring the stone mixture and would miss
that aspect of the job.

Talia turned and marched out of his office. Lacey was in the
break room and started to say something to Talia, but must have
thought twice because of the expression on Talia's face. Lacey
looked from Talia to Dr. Bennett standing behind her and back to
Talia.

"It's been nice knowing you, Lacey. You are the only person
in this place I'll miss." Then Talia grabbed her coat and car keys
and left the office.

She tapped on the passenger side window of the police car
still in the parking lot. "You can go do something more exciting
now. I've been fired and I'm leaving. I'll be at home if you need
me."

On the way home, Talia fantasized about telling Dr. Bennett
and Sally that she was going to tell her brother they were mean to
her and he would make them pay for it.

Then she worried what would happen if he did show up
looking for her there. Obviously, Dr. Bennett and everyone else
out of the loop still thought Brian was a simple embezzler. Even if
she didn't know the scope of it yet, she knew better than to think
anything to do with Brian was at all simple or benign.

She was irritated that she'd spent the gas and time to go to
Grafton to the dental office. Then she thought about how she'd
never have to step foot in there again, never have to hear the
dentist's condescending voice or catch Sally's suspicious glances
in her direction again. But what in the world would she do now?

†

When the phone rang, Talia jumped.

"Relax," Agent Gish said. She counted down on her fingers from three. When no fingers remained up, Talia picked up the receiver and the technician simultaneously pressed two buttons.

Her hand shook slightly as she answered the phone. "Hello."

"Tali." Brian's voice filled the room.

"Brian. What's going on? I tried to call you but the guards wouldn't let me talk to you."

"Oh. Yeah." He laughed. "I've been transferred."

"Transferred? Where?"

"Who's there with you, kiddo?" he said, changing the subject.

"What do you mean?" Talia looked at Gish.

Gish gestured with her hand for her to keep him talking.

"Who is with you?"

Agent Jackson looked out the side of the blinds.

"No one. It's just me."

"You have a tell, you know."

"I have a what?"

"A tell. Something you do that lets me know you aren't being totally honest."

"I do not," Talia said. She knew she sounded defensive.

"Your voice gets slightly higher when you lie. It always has. That's why you were never all that good at it. Well, except for that story about the Gypsies. That was pretty impressive."

"Brian," she interrupted. "Where are you?"

"Talia," he mimicked her tone. "Who is with you?"

"No one," she said, lowering her voice.

He laughed. "Nice try. If I were to come to your door right now, what would I find?"

Talia heard a ding in the background.

"Got to run, sis."

"But, Brian—"

"Tali-Ho," he interrupted.

Talia listened to the dial tone for several moments before Agent Gish said, "Okay, you may hang up now."

"Damn," the technician mumbled.

"Do you really think he knows you're here?" Talia asked.

"He probably just assumes. There's no way he knows. Not for sure, anyway," Jackson said.

Talia thought back to when she and Brian were kids. Once when she'd been put on restriction, Brian called her from various places throughout the weekend. He said it was because he missed her, but it had felt much more like a taunt to Talia. She'd been put on restriction because her dad had caught her stealing her mom's diet pills and she was still on restriction when her dad died.

†

Shay parked her truck in the back of the lot at Talia's apartment building. She was so relieved that the FBI had agreed to let her go to Talia's. Parker promised to increase patrols around the bar while Shay was gone and she trusted he would. Her friend, Brenda, was feeding Poke for her.

As she walked along the sidewalk, Shay thought again about the incident on the parkway with Jeffrey. It had been weighing on her since it happened and she felt guilty that she'd put them both in a dangerous situation. She wasn't sure what she was thinking at the time, other than 'How dare you threaten someone I care about.'

So there it was, an admission to herself that she cared about Talia.

She knocked on the door, and sensed someone looking at her through the peephole before the lock disengaged and the door opened. Shay was surprised by all the electronic boxes with lights and wires coming out every side, even though Talia had described it to her. It seemed also like people were all over the apartment.

Talia was on the sofa with Agents Gish and Jackson. In front of them on the rough wood of the coffee table, they had a spread of food from Taco Bell.

"Sit," Talia said as she scooted over to make room. "Pull up a taco and make yourself comfortable."

Shay smiled. She was glad Talia seemed to be holding up under the circumstances.

Once all the tacos and burritos were consumed, Shay let Talia lead her away from everyone and into the poem room.

Shay immediately noticed the mattress in the corner of the room.

"The agents take turns, in shifts, sleeping in here," Talia said. "I wish I could fast-forward to Brian being found and Jeffrey going to prison so I can relax."

"I know," Shay agreed. She turned to face Talia and placed a hand on the side of her face. "You look tired."

"I am," Talia said, briefly placing her hand over Shay's.

Two more agents came into the apartment and joined Gish and Jackson at the kitchen counter. They spoke in low tones.

Talia watched the agents from the doorway. "I wonder what's up," she whispered.

When Gish looked up from the files and raised an eyebrow, Shay said, "I think we're about to find out."

"Ladies," Jackson said.

Shay and Talia left the poem room and followed the agents to the living room.

"The ballistics came back on the gun from your car," Jackson told Talia. He nodded toward the sofa and Shay and Talia sat close together.

Agent Gish sat on the other side of Talia and Jackson stood on the opposite side of the coffee table.

"We found a match to a homicide on the parkway five years ago," Jackson said.

"A homicide on the parkway?" Talia asked. "I've never heard about a homicide there before Allie and Diane."

"It had originally been reported as an automobile accident. By the time it was discovered the victim had been shot in the head...well...I guess the media had moved on," Gish said.

"Who was the victim?" Shay asked.

Talia grabbed her hand.

"A woman named Bernadette Harris."

Shay looked at Talia for any sign of recognition. Talia shrugged.

"She was a transient with a long history of drug-related arrests. It was assumed her murder was a drug deal gone bad." Gish reached into the folder on the table and pulled out a mug shot.

To Shay, the woman looked well-worn but not unattractive.

Talia gripped Shay's hand tightly and Shay watched as the color drained from her face.

"You know her?" Shay asked.

"That's Bernie. Oh, my God," Talia whispered.

"How do you know Bernadette Harris?" Jackson asked.

"We—ah—" She squeezed her eyes shut. "No, no, no."

"Talia," Shay said, her voice gentle. "Do you want me to go in the other room while you talk about this?"

"No," Talia pleaded. "Please don't go." She looked around the room at the other agents and officers and the technician.

"How about we all take a break," Jackson said to the others. "Let's get some fresh air."

Talia, Shay, and Gish stayed on the sofa as everyone else filed out of the apartment. Shay still held Talia's hand but Talia was focused on the grain of the boards of the table.

"I met Bernie at the beach in Yorktown," Talia said, her voice catching. "We drove around the battlefields in her beat-up Nova while we got stoned."

Gish leafed through the report, read a page, and nodded. "She was found in a Nova that had been stolen."

"After dark, we went to the parkway and parked at the overlook at Ringfield." Talia glanced at Shay then stared down into her lap. "We...ah...we had sex. It was my first time with anyone. She rocked my world and then never called me like she said she would."

Shay swallowed past a lump in her throat.

"I thought I'd done something wrong or wasn't good enough." Talia let got of Shay's hand and wrapped her arms around herself.

They sat quietly for a few minutes. "So that was a federal case since it was on the parkway?" Shay looked at Gish as she spoke. "And nothing else was ever done about it because she was some druggy dyke?"

Gish took a deep breath. "It wasn't my case. I don't know the details of the investigation."

Shay shook her head dismissively. "Were there any prints on the gun?"

Gish nodded. "They matched Jeffrey Gardner."

"Shit," Shay muttered.

"An APB has been issued," Gish said.

"How did Jeffrey's gun end up in Brian's car?" Talia asked.

"Maybe after Jeffrey killed Bernadette, Brian decided to keep the gun for collateral. Or for blackmail," Shay said.

Talia leaned forward with her elbows on her knees and her head in her hands. "Oh, dear God."

†

Talia stood in the poem room and stared at "Soul Dancing" while she waited for Shay to get out of the shower. She was so glad Shay was staying with her for a few days. She loved how Shay showed no sign of judgment over Talia's admission to having sex on the parkway with someone she'd just met.

She thought about Brian's hatred for Ms. Simmons, the gym teacher he had tried to get her to lie about. He was so vehement in his disgust with her that Talia was surprised when he let it drop after she ran away and came back with the Gypsy lie. After that, Talia could never look Ms. Simmons in the eye. Even though she didn't go through with the story, she still felt immense guilt when she saw the teacher. Maybe that was why Brian backed off, because she was no longer a threat to Talia's sexuality since Talia had totally withdrawn from her?

She jumped when the phone rang. She went into the kitchen, and on Agent Gish's count of three, Talia answered.

"The strangest thing happened. I was kidnapped by the CIA and brought to an undisclosed location. I think they are going to try to recruit me as an operative. Do you think I should accept when they do?"

"Brian, where are you?" Talia asked as she glanced at Agent Gish.

"That's where the 'undisclosed location' part is key, my dear. Please, sister, keep up."

Talia recognized the voice, but not the words. Where was the 'Tali' and 'kiddo?'

"Are you there?" Brian asked.

"Tell me what happened." She just wanted her brother to be honest with her once. She wanted him to tell her that he tried to keep Jeffrey from killing Bernie, or that he didn't know about it until after the fact.

"You aren't alone, are you?" He lowered his voice. "I think we are all being watched."

"Brian, what's going on?"

"You tell me."

"Where are you? Are you safe?"

"Of course I'm safe. Are you?" He cleared his throat. "I will keep you safe. I will protect you even if it means protecting you from yourself."

"What does that mean?" Talia asked.

A bell rang. "Oops, got to go."

"Brian, wait," Talia pleaded, but the line was disconnected. She turned toward the technician. "Was he on long enough that time?"

The man looked at Gish and shook his head.

"He really does know we're here," Agent Gish said. "And he's using a timer to keep from getting distracted and staying on the line too long. Damn it."

Talia turned toward movement in the doorway of the kitchen where Shay stood looking concerned. Wanting to lighten things up, Talia struggled to find something clever or cute to say but she came up empty.

There was a knock on the door and Agent Jackson let one of the local cops in. His arms were loaded down with Farm Fresh grocery bags. "Hope you don't mind, but I can't eat any more Taco Bell, pizza, or fast-food burgers. This job is gonna kill us all at this rate."

"What do you have?" Agent Gish asked. "And can you actually cook, because if not, we'll all starve."

Agent Jackson laughed. "Just so you know, sticking some frozen Salisbury steak in the oven isn't actually cooking."

The county guy, Officer Ramos according to his name tag, laughed. "No, sir, I'm going to whip up some chicken enchiladas that will be so good you're gonna cry when they're gone."

"Bring it on," Jackson said.

Talia turned to Agent Gish. "We're going into the other room. Make sure the guys save us some of the enchiladas, okay?"

"I'll try," Gish said, "but you've seen them eat so I can't make any promises."

They went into Talia's bedroom and shut the door. "I'm so used to living alone that having all these people around all the time is driving me a bit batty."

Shay took a step toward the door. "Should I leave? I'm sorry, I didn't even think about adding to the chaos."

Talia reached for Shay's hand. "No, I want you to stay. It's everyone else I wish weren't here."

"They are all trying to keep you safe." Shay squeezed her hand.

"I know and I do appreciate it. I'm just ready for life to get back to normal."

"It will." Shay looked down at the floor. "I guess we need to talk once again about sleeping arrangements?"

"Yeah," Talia laughed. "I guess we do." She led Shay over to the bed and they sat on the end of it. "I vote that we sleep together in my bed."

Shay coughed.

"I mean sleep. Just sleep. Anything else would be too weird with everyone else here."

"Yes, it would. I wouldn't even think about—okay, maybe I would *think* about it, but that's all."

"That settles it?"

"Yes, that settles it," Shay agreed.

Talia inhaled deeply. "Do you smell that?"

"How could I not? Wow! It's going to be delicious."

"Maybe we should go back out there to keep from missing it," Talia said.

"Yes, let's. I haven't seen them eat but I'll take Angela's word for it."

"So, how do you know Angela Gish?"

Shay pursed her lips, then smiled. "Well, we were both at a crime scene one night. My gaydar was pinging all over the place. Later when she was at the station picking up a perp, I let out a hint or two about us both being family."

"Why are you blushing?" Talia asked.

"Because my gaydar was wrong, and she didn't have a clue as to what I was talking about. Then it finally sank in, and let's just say it was a bit awkward."

"But then you two became good friends and laugh about it all the time?"

"No, then I saw her outside the FBI field office in Norfolk when I went to talk to Agent Jackson after we found the stuff stashed in your car. We recognized each other and got to talking."

"So, she forgave you for your broken gaydar?"

"Nope." Shay chuckled. "She told me that she'd come out to herself a couple of months after that little incident. She was gay but she just didn't know it yet."

Talia laughed, then sniffed the air again. "We can't take the chance of missing that food."

"No we can't," Shay said as she followed Talia out of the bedroom.

"Damn, they did come back out," Jackson said. "That means we have to share."

Thirty minutes later, Officer Ramos was spooning out chicken enchiladas and smiling at all the compliments. Talia dipped a forkful into a smidgen of sour cream on her plate and stuck it in her mouth. After swallowing, she said, "I hope this doesn't ruin me for Taco Bell. Hey, Officer Ramos, do you want to come over and cook for me once a week?"

Talia couldn't help but adore the blush from Ramos or be aware of how Shay put her hand on her shoulder in what Talia hoped was an effort to stake her claim.

When everyone finished eating, Talia made them leave the kitchen so she could have some alone-time with the dishes. Several people offered to help but Talia shooed them out. She took her time, enjoying the comfort of the sudsy, hot water as she scrubbed sauce off the plates and forks. When she finished, she met Shay back in the poem room.

"Dee wants that red "No" poem we talked about," Shay said. "Everything went a little crazy so I forgot to tell you she said she wants to buy one for the bar, and something else for her home. She'll let you know which one for her house later."

"Oh, wow." Talia traced the word 'woman' with her fingertip on the canvas Dee wanted for the bar. "That's great."

Jackson cleared his throat in the doorway. "I was thinking about crashing in here for a few hours—"

"Oh, I am so sorry," Talia said.

"I meant to tell you that I think your poem things are really cool," Jackson added, blushing slightly as he spoke.

"Thank you," Talia said, smiling as she turned to leave. "I appreciate you saying that."

Talia shut the bedroom door behind her, then joined Shay on the end of the bed. "What's new with Kate? Has her mother called her or anything?" she asked.

"No, not since the last time I talked to Kate," Shay said. "She did tell me that April checked herself into the hospital."

"Oh, thank God. Now she can get some help."

"Yeah."

"I really was hoping that Kate, April, and their mom would connect for more than just that one day."

Shay pulled her close. "You are one of the most compassionate people I know."

Talia smiled and let her body melt into Shay's. Nothing had ever felt so good but she abruptly pulled away.

"Something wrong?" Shay asked.

"I...ah...I don't think I should be touching you in any capacity before crawling into bed with you."

Shay nodded. "I do believe you're on to something. Are you tired now?"

"A little. But maybe not tired enough to be able to fall to sleep right away." She glanced toward the dresser. "You want to play cards? We could get ready for bed, then play cards until we're really tired."

"Okay. What should we play?" Shay got up and walked to where her overnight bag sat in the corner. She pulled out a pair of boxers and a T-shirt.

"Poker?" Talia asked.

"Okay, I'll go into the bathroom to change and you can change out here."

A few minutes later, they sat across from one another on the bed and played five card draw. Talia was losing terribly. She told herself it was because sitting across the bed from Shay while she wore boxers was way too distracting for her to keep her head in the game. She glanced down at herself, at her flowered pajama bottoms and Cyndi Lauper tour shirt.

"You need to work on your poker face," Shay said. "I can read you like a book."

"My brother always said I had the worst poker face." Brian had also said on the phone that she had a 'tell' when she lied. She couldn't think of any way she could tell when her brother lied. He was so good at it, it scared her.

Once they were exhausted, they hunkered down under the covers, not touching. Talia knew she'd never fall to sleep if she stayed this keyed up and attuned to every breath Shay took. But, when she least expected it, she drifted off.

Talia was awakened by thrashing beside her. She rolled toward Shay and just missed getting an elbow in the face. "Whoa," she said in a low voice. "Shay, wake up, you're having a bad dream."

Shay bolted straight up into a sitting position on the bed. She was sweating and trembling.

"It's okay," Talia reassured her. "It's okay, you're here with me. You're safe."

Shay took several deep breaths.

"Come here," Talia said as she opened her arms. She was pleasantly surprised when Shay settled in against her and drifted back to sleep.

Chapter Eleven

Ramos was making ham and cheese omelets when Talia and Shay came out of the bedroom the next morning. Agent Jackson was sitting on the sofa reading the newspaper and Gish was sleeping in the poem room.

"It smells incredible," Talia told Ramos.

The phone rang and Jackson put down the paper and walked into the kitchen. He pushed the button on the ever-present equipment and called out to the technician in the bathroom. "George, it's show-time!"

George rushed out, drying his hands.

Jackson did the silent countdown from three and Talia answered the phone.

"Hello?"

"How are you, little sister?"

"Brian, where are you?"

"I'm still hanging out with the CIA. These people are a hoot. Did you sleep well last night?"

"Yeah." She looked at Agent Gish, who had just joined them. Gish gave her a keep it going gesture. "I slept fine. How about you?"

"I see your girlfriend stayed over."

Talia glanced at Shay.

"How cute, a pajama party," Brian continued. "So, now, here is when I have to protect you from yourself. You see, you can't let that woman drag you down. It's not natural, and I can't have you acting like that."

"Brian..." Talia hesitated when she heard the bell go off. Afraid he'd hang up, she let the words rush out. "Brian, there's nothing you can do about us being together. Nothing."

"Oh, you think not?"

"Yeah, I think not. I'm beginning to think you're just a bully that's full of hot air. A lying bully who will never get the chance to determine how I live my life."

"How about I kill your girlfriend? Then we can discuss it further."

Talia felt the burn of bile at the back of her throat. Who was this person? How could he possibly say that about any human being, let alone someone she cared so much for? She turned toward the others when she saw a lot of movement behind her. By the looks on their faces, she figured they must have gotten the trace. "There's nothing to discuss, Brian."

"Tali-ho. And I sure will enjoy killing her slowly."

The line went dead.

"We got him," Gish said. "Good job, Talia, good job."

Talia looked around and smiled when she saw everyone else was smiling. "Hey," she said as she took Shay's hand. "We'll get him now." They embraced.

"Holy shit," Jackson said. "This address is in here...he's in an apartment right across the parking lot."

Officer Ramos spoke into his radio, calling for backup. Gish and Jackson both pulled on their bulletproof vests and headed to the door. Talia ran out behind them, ignoring Shay's plea for her to stay in the apartment.

Talia knew Shay was right on her heels. She ran as fast as she could, catching up to Gish and Jackson just as they broke down the door to Maybe Lesbian's apartment. Shay and Ramos held her back at the broken doorway, while the others searched the apartment. Talia's gaze fell on her neighbor, sitting in an overstuffed chair with a cord around her neck. A blanket was spread over her legs and her hands were in her lap. If not for the cord and the fact that she was blue and lifeless, it would appear she

147

was just watching TV. Talia felt her legs start to go out from under her.

"I've got you, I've got you," Shay said as she held onto Talia.

"Clear!" Jackson called from inside the apartment. "Shit, what are they doing here?" He looked at Talia and Shay, then pointed at Ramos. "Get them both back to Talia's apartment and have someone on them at all times."

Talia's next thought was how cold it seemed in the apartment and how cold she felt looking at Maybe Lesbian, knowing it was her fault that she was dead. "Oh, my God!" Talia cried out.

Shay and Ramos pressed in close to Talia and someone handed them two bulletproof vests. Shay slipped one on Talia before putting on her own.

As they started across the street to Talia's apartment, Talia became aware that there were heavily-armed agents and police stationed everywhere around her apartment complex.

Once inside, Talia went to the window and moved the curtains to the side. She had a clear view of Maybe Lesbian's apartment and all of the police. She heard words like lockdown and safe house being tossed about by some of the officers.

She turned to Ramos. "What was her name?"

"The victim?" He shrugged. "I don't know yet."

Talia and Shay both turned to look at Agent Gish as she came into Talia's apartment. "Did they catch him?" Talia asked.

Gish shook her head. "We'll go through every apartment, one by one. We've got roadblocks up all around town. We'll get him."

This time, Talia asked Gish. "What was her name?"

"Linda Adams. Did you know her?"

"Just in passing. We spoke a few times and waved when we saw each other coming and going. I'd forgotten her name, or maybe never knew it," Talia said, the last words coming out with a sob.

"It's okay," Shay said as she wrapped her arms around Talia. "It's going to be all right."

"Okay, time to go. Pack your clothes and toiletries only," Jackson said.

"But my poems—"

"I'll see to it that they get over there to you," Agent Gish said. She looked at Shay. "You go with them and I'll get your truck to you later."

"Where are we going?" Talia asked.

"To a safe house in Norfolk where he won't find you. We'll keep someone on your apartment in the meantime, but we're pretty sure he's gone."

"Why do you say that? Where do you think he would go?"

"There was a Pennsylvania address near the phone," Jackson said.

"Mom," Talia whispered. "Would he go after our mom?" She directed the question to Shay, but didn't give her time to answer. "He would. We have to warn her."

"The local police are going there to check on her now. They'll keep her and her family safe, and keep an eye out for Brian."

Talia grew dizzy with the amount of activity. After she packed a suitcase with clothes and toiletries, she sat on the arm of the sofa and closed her eyes.

Arms wrapped around her. The scent of vanilla comforted her. "Oh, Shay," she whispered.

"We'll get through this. I promise we will."

"He said he was going to kill you. And then I kept pushing him and made him mad enough that he really will try. What have I done?"

"What you did was think fast on your feet. You did it. You kept him on the phone long enough to get the trace. Now we have him on the run," Shay said.

"And we have no idea where he is or if he's still watching."

"Talia," Gish said as she approached them.

Shay pulled away from Talia.

"Here's what will happen next," Gish said. "We will move both of you to a safe house in Norfolk." She turned to Shay. "Tell the officers what you want from your house and they will go get it and bring it to you. You will both need to stay in the safe house until we get the situation under control."

"Poke," Shay said. "Tell them to get my cat, Poke." Her voice quivered slightly.

†

Shay and Talia walked through the safe house to get a feel for the layout. There were three bedrooms and two baths.

"How should we do this?" Talia asked.

Shay studied her face, noticing the dark puffiness beneath Talia's eyes. "How do you want to do it?"

"I would rather we stay in the same room. I feel safe with you." Talia looked away as she spoke.

"Then that settles it." Shay led her into the master bedroom. They placed their bags on the love seat in the corner of the room. "Sleeping here together leaves the other two bedrooms for the agents or whoever they have staying with us."

Voices came from the kitchen as Gish and Jackson spoke to two other agents. Shay was glad that it looked like there would only be the FBI, no local police officers. It wasn't that she didn't have faith in her ex-department; she just didn't think it was good to have those distracting dynamics, all things considered.

Jackson looked up as they went back into the living room area. "Shay, have you checked out the garage?"

She glanced toward the door he indicated. "Why, is my new Corvette in there?"

Jackson grinned. "Well, now it'll be anticlimactic. Thanks a lot."

Shay opened the door that led from the laundry room to the garage and turned on the lights. She smiled at the sight of a fully equipped gym, complete with punching bag. "Oh, very nice," she said. She hoped the treadmill in the corner would help Talia feel a little less restless.

"Shay, Talia," Gish called from the kitchen. They met her in there. "The phone is in here on the wall. It should be limited to official or emergency use only."

They both nodded.

"The house is secure. Don't open or unlock any of the windows. Don't go outside. We will have an agent in here with you, but you won't be tripping all over us anymore. Additional agents are in the neighborhood. You are safe in here, as long as you don't contact anyone to let them know where you are."

"May I call my mom? She'll be wondering why I haven't called lately." Shay felt a pit in her stomach at the thought of her parents worrying about her.

"Yes, but don't tell her where you are...or say anything about what's going on."

Shay nodded. She was about to ask Talia if she wanted to call her mom, then remembered they didn't talk regularly and that her mom was probably now also in protective custody. She thought of her friends and knew they would be worrying. "I almost hate to ask, but can I at least call Dee at the bar and tell her to tell everyone we're okay?"

Agent Gish smiled. "Tell your friends you are okay, but please, don't let anything slip."

Shay was about to comment on Gish's lack of faith in her but, on further thought, decided to stay quiet.

The others went into the living room and Shay stayed behind in the kitchen to use the phone. "Hi, Mom." As soon as the words were out she thought about what her mom had told her not too long before about 'Hi, Mom' meaning something was up, and 'Hey, there,' meaning all was right in the world. "And nothing is up."

"Hmph. When you were an itty-bitty thing, you lied about a stray dog you *just had no idea that it'd followed you home.* Your dad and I knew you'd probably coaxed it along. Anyway, by the end of the day the guilt of lying was eating at you so badly that you came into our bedroom crying and fessed up."

"You still let me keep the dog."

"Of course we did. Now, what's up?"

"I met someone." She swallowed hard. "But it's so early on and I don't want to jinx it by talking about her."

"You're practically whispering. Is she with you now?"

"Yes."

"Are you happy?"

She glanced around the home that wasn't hers and was surprised when she answered, "Yes."

"Then when you're ready you'll tell us all about her."

"Of course. So, how's Dad?"

"Still deafer than a doorknob and too stubborn to do anything about it."

Shay smiled at the familiarity of her mom's words. She couldn't wait for all of this to be behind them so she could introduce Talia to her parents.

After hanging up, Shay stuck her head out of the kitchen. "Talia, do you want to come in while I call Dee?"

Talia joined Shay in the kitchen. "Should you call Kate, too?"

Shay looked at her watch. "Kate won't be home, but I could leave her a quick message that we've gone on vacation."

Talia cocked her head.

"I know, lying." She shrugged. "It's for everyone's own good." She dialed Kate's number and left her a vague message about being out of town with Talia and that they'd call again when they returned.

Talia kissed her cheek. "You're pretty good at that," she teased. "Just don't ever lie to me for my own good, okay?"

"Okay." Shay gave Talia a quick peck on the lips then dialed the phone again. Dee answered the bar's office phone on the first ring. "Hey, Dee, it's Shay."

"Oh, my God, Shay. Where have you been?"

"I'm out of town with Talia. We'll be back soon."

"Did you see on the news about that woman being murdered in Newport News? Kate said that's Talia's neighborhood."

Shay could hear the door to the office opening. There was a rustling, then Lana's voice boomed into the phone. "Shay, oh God. You're with Talia? They're looking for her brother. They think he killed her neighbor after escaping from prison."

There was another rustling, then Dee came back on the line. "That's why you're out of town isn't it? Where are you? Are you safe?"

Talia whispered, "What's she saying?"

"Yes, we are safe," Shay said. "Here," she held the phone out to Talia, "say hello."

"Hi, Dee."

"Talia? Is it true? Did your brother murder your neighbor?"

"I can't get into all that right now. Just know that we are safe."

Shay took the receiver back from Talia. "Listen, we really have to go. I just wanted you and Lana and Kate to know that we're okay."

"Be careful," Dee said before Shay disconnected the phone.

Shay glanced toward the doorway and saw Gish walk away. Of course she'd be listening to make sure they didn't screw up and say too much.

"I'm going to see what I can scare up for dinner," Shay said to Talia. "Why don't you go relax?"

Shay scanned the groceries in the fridge and decided to make sloppy joes for everyone. It might not be a gourmet meal, but at least it wasn't being eaten out of a box or bag.

Her efforts were much appreciated by Talia, Jackson, and Gish and, after eating, they decided to all work out together. The camaraderie made Shay feel like she did after first joining the police force. She smiled as she watched Talia try to figure out the treadmill. "May I?" she asked.

Talia stepped away. "Please do."

Shay explained the settings to her and then stood back and watched Talia's first tentative steps. "There you go," Shay said enthusiastically.

Jackson and Shay took turns spotting each other on the free weights while Talia stayed on the treadmill and Gish terrorized the punching bag. After they started to wrap up their workout, Shay asked Jackson, "Any word on Poke?"

"Nope, not yet. He's been quite elusive but they'll get him."

"I hope they aren't scaring him," Shay muttered. "Maybe I should go get him."

Agent Jackson shook his head. "Nice try, but you stay put. I promise you they will be gentle and not scare him."

"First dibs on the shower," Talia called as she took off out of the garage.

Shay watched her and thought how much she wished she was joining Talia in the shower. *Stop it*, she told herself. *No use in getting worked up in that way now.*

✝

Shay sat up in bed and struggled to catch her breath. Finally she turned to look at Talia, also sitting up in bed and wide-eyed.

"Another nightmare?" Talia whispered.

"Yeah, sorry."

"You don't have to be sorry. Have you tried talking to someone about them?"

Shay shook her head, knowing she didn't want to talk to anyone about them. Or did she? She held open her arms and Talia snuggled in with her.

"I'm a good listener," Talia whispered.

"I know you are, sweetie. I just don't want to fill your head with my images."

"It would be okay. Maybe sharing your images would help dilute them."

Shay held on to Talia's hand as she rolled over, bringing Talia with her to spoon Shay from behind. "Are you sure?" Shay's question came out ragged and raw.

"Yes, tell me, but only if you want."

They held each other in silence for a long time. Shay began to fear Talia had fallen back to sleep but then Talia kissed the back of her head.

Shay struggled for words for a few more moments and then began to speak. "During my interrogation, the agent made me look at pictures of Allie and Diane." She shook. "It was so horrible. The photos were so graphic and the worst part is Allie was my friend." The last words were a half-whisper.

"I am so sorry," Talia whispered.

"He kept accusing me of killing them and pushing the pictures back in my face...and he screamed at me to look at the jagged cuts and the blood dried on them." She squeezed Talia's hand. "No one should have to look at something like that. No one."

Talia held on to her, pressing against her back, burying her face in Shay's neck. "I'm sorry."

"So often when I close my eyes I see Allie and Diane all broken and bloody. And the nightmares are confusing. Sometimes it's them I see, and sometimes it's other people." Her body convulsed with the memory of seeing Talia's face in the carnage in her dreams. "Sometimes I walk up to a car on the parkway and look in the window and it's Dee or Kate or…or you."

Talia held her tighter. "It's okay, it's okay."

Shay cried herself to sleep in Talia's arms. When she awoke, she was alone in the bed. She got up, took care of her morning routine and then joined Talia in the kitchen.

"What'cha doing?" Shay asked in a sing-song voice.

"Trying to figure out the toaster. Technology and I don't get along, as you saw with the treadmill." She turned around and gave Shay a shy smile. "You okay?"

"I am better, but I'm sorry about last night."

Talia closed the distance between them and wrapped her arms around Shay. "There's nothing to be sorry about. You know you can talk to me about anything."

They jumped at the sound of a throat being cleared behind them. "Any coffee?" Jackson asked.

"Not yet. Give us just a minute." She took Talia by the hand. "Today you learn to make coffee and toast."

"Should I be afraid?" Jackson asked.

"Yes," Talia answered. "Be afraid…be very afraid."

There was a knock at the door and Jackson left the kitchen. Shay heard a woman's voice and made out one word. "Cat."

Jackson stood in the doorway to the kitchen holding a pet carrier. "You have a visitor, Shay."

"Poke," she said. She held out her hands to take the carrier.

"Should you take him to the bedroom and give him a chance to acclimate?" Talia asked.

"Yeah." She glanced around the kitchen. "It's all yours," she told Jackson.

Shay closed the bedroom door behind her and put the carrier on the floor. She opened the wire door and sat on the floor beside it, leaning against the love seat. "Hey, Pokey, you okay?"

He let out a little grunt, stuck his head through the carrier opening and looked around. "Hi, Poke. I'm sorry I had to leave you all alone but we're together now."

She smiled as he immediately began to purr and climbed into her lap.

"That's my boy. Your friend Talia is also here." He head-butted her chin and she laughed. "Yeah, I like her too."

†

Talia wiggled her toe and watched as Poke stalked it. He crouched low, moved in slow motion, wriggled his rear end and then pounced. Talia moved her foot just in time.

"He's going to get that toe of yours eventually, you know," Shay said.

"I know."

"And he has teeth and claws, you know."

"I know." Talia narrowed her eyes at Poke. "You wouldn't, would you?"

"Oh, yes, he would," Shay answered for him. She had a towel draped around her neck and her hair was still after-shower wet.

"You're going to miss teaching your self-defense class today," Talia said.

"Yeah, I talked to Parker and he knows of a woman who can fill in for me until—well, until we get all of this sorted out."

Agent Jackson came into the living room and sat on the edge of the sofa. As he tied his running shoes, he said, "I'm going for a run. There's an agent out front attempting to look like a landscaper. Call the emergency number by the phone if anything comes up. You know, since you'll be here in the house alone for a couple of hours."

"That was subtle," Shay said after he left.

Talia laughed but as soon as they were alone she grew nervous. She jumped up. "I'm gonna get in the shower."

Talia lathered and rinsed her hair quickly, then moved slower while soaping her body. The flesh between her legs grew thick with anticipation as she washed there. She rinsed off and hurried to get dry. She stood in the bathroom and stared at the shorts and T-shirt she'd placed on the side of the sink to change into. Should she be bold and walk out with nothing on? She took a deep breath and knew she wouldn't. She slipped into the clothing and out of the bathroom.

Shay was sitting on the edge of the bed in a tank top and boxers. Talia swallowed hard at the sheer sexiness emanating from her. "Wow."

"Wow?" Shay asked.

"We are alone. We have some privacy, finally."

"What would you like to do with this privacy?"

Talia looked down at her shorts and T-shirt. "Something that would entail losing some of this clothing?"

"Sounds perfect." Shay stood up and pulled the covers down.

Talia slipped out of her clothes and stepped closer to Shay. Shay undressed and pulled her into her arms and when their skin touched Talia had a fleeting thought about melting into Shay. She shivered and then marveled at how perfect they fit together and how incredible it felt to both her flesh and mind. She quivered.

"Is this okay?" Shay whispered.

Talia inhaled the scent of vanilla. "This is perfect," she answered.

Shay's hands moved down Talia's sides and sent a burning ache surging between her legs. Talia kissed Shay's neck and slid her hands up Shay's muscular back.

"Let's get in bed," Shay said.

They slid under the sheets and Shay rolled on top of Talia. "Tell me what you like."

Talia couldn't get the words out. She had waited so long to feel Shay pressed against her like she was that now she couldn't even speak.

Shay kissed her long and deep while her hands moved up and down Talia's sides.

Talia grabbed Shay's hand and guided it between her legs. "Please," she whispered and gasped as Shay's fingers found her wetness.

"You're so wet. So beautifully wet," Shay murmured.

Talia pressed upward, forcing Shay's touch to press more firmly. "Yes." Talia sighed.

Shay pressed two fingers inside of her. "Do you like that?" she whispered.

"Yes." Talia breathed deep as Shay's fingers moved faster and harder against her. "I do, I do like that, but—but—"

"Tell me what you want."

"Your mouth…please, I want your mouth on me," Talia answered.

Shay moved down the length of Talia, kissing her as she went. Her mouth found the wetness between Talia's legs and she stroked Talia with her tongue.

"Oh, yes." Talia held on tight as Shay's mouth moved in and around her wetness until her body quaked and exploded into orgasm.

Shay moved back up to be able to look her in the eyes.

"So long," Talia whispered. "I've wanted you for so long."

Shay held her tight. "You are so beautiful."

Talia smiled. "Oh, but you are wonderful. And now I want to show you just how much I think you are." She rolled on top of Shay and let her hands and mouth prove it.

Chapter Twelve

"I can't believe it's been a week and there's still no sign of Jeffrey or Brian," Talia said.

Shay pulled her against her and kissed her neck. "We should get up soon."

"Yeah. Is it just me, or are Jackson's runs getting longer and longer." She couldn't help smiling at that.

"I think he hangs out longer on the porch." Shay sat up and pulled on her T-shirt. "He is a good guy. At least we didn't get stuck with some macho jerk staying here with us."

"Yeah." Talia got out of bed and got dressed. "We really are lucky." She fought against tears.

"Oh, sweetie," Shay said as she got up and embraced her. "What is it?"

"Tomorrow's Christmas and for a minute I felt sorry for us that we can't really celebrate it, but then I thought about Allie and Diane and their families. Oh and my neighbor, Linda." Talia cried, tears dampening Shay's shirt.

Shay held her tighter.

"I don't need a Christmas tree or presents. I don't need any of that, but I do wish there could be closure for the families. I wish they would catch whoever killed Allie and Diane. And I wish they would catch Jeffrey for what he did to Bernie, and Brian for what he did to Linda." Sobs shook her body.

"I know, I know," Shay said. "It will happen. All of that will happen."

They jumped at the door opening and closing loudly. "Ho, ho, ho," Jackson's voice boomed through the house.

Shay led the way out of the bedroom. Jackson and Gish were struggling to get a Christmas tree into the den. "Merry Christmas," Gish sang out.

"Merry Christmas," Talia echoed, feeling a little giddy at the sight of the tree.

"We have some boxes of decorations we'll bring in too." Jackson looked around the den. "How about putting it in that corner?"

"Should be good," Shay said. "You aren't planning to put anything on that tree that's breakable, are you? Poke is quite the rascal this time of year."

Gish's mouth twisted in thought. "There's nothing in the box that will be a problem if it breaks. We should skip the tinsel though."

"Yeah," Shay agreed. "Not safe for cats. Oh, and no poinsettias either, I'm afraid."

"I never would have thought about those things. Good thing I didn't trust myself to have any pets, huh?" Talia asked.

"Don't worry, I'll make you cat savvy yet," Shay said to Talia.

Talia stared at Shay while she and the others positioned the tree in the corner of the room. Shay's statement had sounded a lot like a promise to Talia, a promise of a future. *Yes*, she thought, *this is going to be the best Christmas ever.*

After the tree was decorated, Poke went about exploring it thoroughly. Gish broke out some eggnog. "Sorry it's nonalcoholic."

"Are you kidding? I want you both at your sober best to protect us from all the boogie men out there." As soon as she said it, Talia wished she hadn't. It had almost seemed like a normal Christmas Eve up to reminding herself and the others that it was anything but.

"Aren't you guys going to spend the holiday with your families?" Shay asked.

"I'll stay with you tonight," Jackson said. "Then I'll get to spend the day tomorrow with my family while Angela stays here." He turned to Talia. "Hey, I was wondering if I could buy the poem about dancing from you. My sister would love it and I can never figure out the right gift for her and her partner."

"Yes, I would be honored if you gave your sister one of my paintings." She felt tingly thinking about someone else enjoying her poem painting.

"Great, I'll take it with me tomorrow for my family's get-together."

As elated as she was about the painting, Talia felt sad that Gish and Jackson had to split up their time during the holidays in order to protect her and Shay. Not that she didn't appreciate it, but she just wished it wasn't necessary.

She thought about the last Christmas her father was alive. It was another of his over-the-top holiday meals. Then she thought about Thanksgiving dinner with Brian a month earlier, when he told Talia the story about their dad getting angry at her. She felt a little sick, not knowing if it was just another one of Brian's lies.

Why did he do it? she wondered. *Why did he lie so much?* She could remember when they were growing up and their mom would lie to their dad to keep them out of trouble. Once when Talia asked her mom why she always did that, her mom's response was, "Why shouldn't I? Why should he be able to put you two on restriction just to go away for work and leave me stuck with you whining and crying about being home?" At the time, the answer to her question didn't faze her. Now, after all that had happened, from her dad's death, to her mom's leaving for a new life, and now this thing with Brian, she thought it was no big surprise they were all such messed-up Liarheads.

Well, Talia was living a new life. A life without lying and a life with Shay. She watched as Shay grabbed the newspaper from the kitchen counter and took it into the den to read. Talia never read the paper, unless she was looking for a specific story, and the fact that Shay always did made her seem so much more like an adult than Talia would ever feel.

Talia grabbed her notepad and pen. She'd been working on a poem about Shay that she had titled "Vanilla."

When Shay muttered, "Whoa," Talia sat down next to her and read over Shay's shoulder. The newspaper article was about Officers Dixon and McCoy—the same officers who'd claimed Paulie had resisted arrest when they assaulted him—getting caught beating up another gay man. This time there was security camera footage and several witnesses.

"Feel vindicated?" Talia asked.

"No, just sad and angry." Shay held up the paper. "Look at what page the article is on."

Talia saw it was almost at the back of the news section. "But it's better than nothing, right?"

"Do you think we'll always have to accept 'better than nothing'?" Shay asked.

Talia massaged Shay's shoulders and thought about how Allie and Diane were relegated to back pages as well and how Bernie never really made the pages at all. "I sure hope not."

Shay leaned forward slightly. "I'll give you all day to stop doing that."

Talia smiled, then kissed the top of Shay's head. She rubbed Shay's tight muscles and thought about touching her in a more intimate way and felt herself grow wet. "Wow," she whispered.

"Wow, what?" Shay asked. She turned around to look at Talia. "Why is your face so red?"

Talia laughed. "Use your imagination."

Shay gestured for her to lean down and when Talia did, Shay whispered in her ear, "I'd like to use more than just my imagination."

Talia's breath caught in her chest. "Yes."

†

Shay hung up the phone after talking to her parents and wishing them a Merry Christmas. She'd just walked back into the den when the phone rang. Talia and Shay both jumped. Shay wondered how long it would be before they quit associating the ringing of the phone with Brian's sick game of cat and mouse. When Jackson answered the phone, he did so with his back to them. When he turned to face them after a lot of "I sees" and "ah ha's" his expression was unreadable. "Yes, they're right here."

Shay smiled. As if they could be anywhere else. She glanced at Talia, who had quit reading her novel and spread the tattered copy of *Rubyfruit Jungle* opened on her lap as she watched Jackson.

Jackson thanked the caller and hung up. He took his time freshening up his coffee before making his way into the den and sitting on the chair across from where Shay and Talia sat close on the sofa.

"What's up?" Talia asked.

"Hampton PD found Jeffrey Gardner's van."

"Oh?" Shay asked. "And what about him?"

"Inconclusive right now. The van was found in the parking lot of an abandoned auto shop. It had been burned up."

"And they're sure it's his van?" Talia asked.

"Yes. It's a dark blue, 1983 Chevy G20 diesel and the VIN matched. There are badly burned human remains inside the van. Hopefully they'll be able to tell conclusively whether or not it's Gardner."

"Wow," Talia whispered. "Was it foul play?"

"Are you asking if we think Brian found him first?" Jackson asked.

"Well, if not Brian, than someone else he's pissed off. My brother can't possibly be the only person who has an ax to grind with this guy."

Shay wondered if Talia knew how much it sounded like she was defending her brother. When Talia looked away quickly and wouldn't look at either Shay or Jackson, Shay figured she did.

A few hours later when the phone rang again, Shay followed Jackson into the kitchen. She watched Talia from the doorway and was pretty sure she was pretending to read. This time Jackson only spoke for a second before hanging up and turning to Shay.

"They found part of Gardner's wallet and driver's license on the body. It was charred but still readable. They'll still try to get DNA from the remains, but there's no real reason to think it's not him."

Shay nodded. "Now we have to find Brian." She didn't take her eyes off Talia as she spoke.

"Is she going to be okay?" Jackson asked.

"I sure hope so," she whispered. Shay couldn't even begin to imagine how it would be to find out that someone you'd known and loved your whole life was a monster. She couldn't even begin to comprehend what that could do to someone.

†

"I can't believe there are only a few hours left in 1986." Shay plopped down on the sofa, close to Talia.

"I can't believe we've been squirreled away in this house for two weeks," Talia countered.

"It hasn't been all bad, has it?" Shay asked.

Talia snuggled in closer. "No. I especially like Jackson's runs." She felt her face warming and smiled into Shay's neck.

"Yeah, me too." Shay laughed. "Do you think he normally runs this much, or is he doing it to give us a lot of...private time?"

"I don't know." Talia squeezed Shay's leg. "Are you making any New Year's resolutions?"

"No, I never keep them anyway," Shay answered. "How about you?"

"I'm resolving to keep working on the honesty thing."

Shay smiled. "You've been doing great as far as I can tell."

"Thank you. I'm also resolving not to let my brother keep me prisoner too much longer."

Shay took her hand. "We have to stay here and wait for them to find Brian. Our number one priority has to be to stay safe."

"I know that. I really do. But I am so ready to start living a normal life. I feel so bad that you've been stuck in this limbo because of me."

"Things will get back to normal in time," Shay said. "And there is no place I would rather be than with you."

165

"You don't resent this situation—or me—even just a little?"

"None of this is your fault." She turned Talia's face to look her in the eyes. "You know that, don't you?"

"In theory I know it, but I just don't want to lose you."

Shay hugged her. "The first thing I want to do when we can go out is to dance with you in front of everyone at the bar."

"Oh, yeah? What else are you going to do in front of everyone?"

"Kiss you just like this." She pressed her lips against Talia's.

There was a rustling behind them and Jackson muttered, "Oh, sorry."

"Hi," they said in unison.

"Shay, do you think you could spot me?"

"Yeah, sure." She turned to Talia. "You up for some workout time?"

"Let me go put on my running shoes." She jumped up and headed to their bedroom to put on the new Reeboks Agent Gish had brought her.

Once in the garage, Talia set the treadmill on a relatively slow speed to start. She increased the incline until she felt a pleasant pull on her legs and butt, then she turned up the speed a touch and settled into a rhythm. She watched Shay spot Jackson as he bench-pressed some very heavy weights. Shay glanced at her and smiled. Talia would never get tired of being on the receiving end of that smile.

She increased the speed slightly and started to jog. Her dad's smile flashed through her mind from a long time ago. Too quickly his smile disappeared and she saw an expression of disappointment and then pain. She closed her eyes and it was as if a highlight reel of her relationship with her father was playing on a screen in front of her.

Talia was a daddy's girl when she was very young. Up until she was about eight years old, she had tried so hard to please him. She mimicked him by trying to walk like him, talk like him, and smell like him. Finally she quit sneaking his Old Spice and seeking his attention. She had lied to him about eating the last of the cheesecake. Brian knew she'd lied and that was the first time he had showed any interest in her. For some reason, once Brian started to pay attention to her, she couldn't seem to break away and regain her father's affection.

There were some rough spots in her relationship with her brother, like the thing with Timmy and Tommy when she was ten and Brian wouldn't stick up for her because she'd backed down on her lie. But for the most part, though, Brian was her best friend and ally.

Her father's expression of sadness flashed through her mind. She increased the speed on the treadmill yet again, forcing herself to run hard, trying to outpace her dad's disappointment. She remembered backing Brian's story when he'd lied to their dad about the goldfish that had disappeared and wondered if he'd known then how he'd lost his daughter to his son.

Her dad's sadness and disappointment turned into slack, expressionless flesh as he lay in the bathtub, lifeless. But was he really lifeless? Could she have saved him if she had told someone?

She could hear the pounding of her feet on the treadmill and something else...her own anguished sobbing.

She stepped off the moving belt and onto the stationary sides and, with shoulders hunched, she let the tears course unchecked down her face. She flipped the switch and, when the treadmill belt stopped, she stumbled off and ran out of the garage gym. She could hear Shay calling from behind her but kept going until she was in the bathroom they shared. She turned the water as hot as she could stand it and stood in the shower and cried until no more tears would come.

After she dried off, she dressed in jeans and a long-sleeved T-shirt. She found Shay sitting on the sofa reading the newspaper. Shay looked up and patted the cushion next to her. "Sit with me," she said.

Talia sat beside her.

"You okay?"

She gave a negative shake of her head.

"Would it help to talk about it?"

Talia nodded. "I need to. I can't say my resolution to be honest is legitimate if I'm hiding something important from you."

Shay cocked her head.

Talia's hands shook. "This is the hardest thing I've ever had to tell someone." She stared at the carpet on the floor in front of her and took a deep breath.

"It's okay, sweetheart. Really it is. Tell me what's going on."

"The day my dad died...I found his body in the bathtub..."

"Oh, sweetie, I'm sorry, I didn't realize you'd found him."

"I found him floating in the tub. He was kind of bloated and bluish white." She took several deep breaths. "I saw him there and I turned around, shut the door, and pretended not to."

Shay stared at her. "I don't understand."

"I found my dad hours before my mom did and I just went back into my room, got in bed, and pretended that I hadn't seen anything." She looked at Shay for a long moment. "He might have still been alive and I might have been able to get him help. He might still be alive if I had just said something."

"Oh."

"I was embarrassed and ashamed and selfish."

"You were young," Shay said.

"Not that young. I was thirteen and definitely old enough to know better." She moved a few inches away from Shay. "I've never asked my mom about that day or about whether anyone knew how long he'd been there."

"Do you want me to dig around to see what I can find out?"

Talia shrugged. "I don't know if I could handle knowing for sure that my father is dead because of me."

"Oh, sweetie." Shay pulled her closer.

"He'd gotten mad at me for something a few days earlier and threatened to send me away. Maybe I wanted him to die."

"You don't *really* believe that, do you?" Shay asked.

"No. Not really." Talia's tears flowed. "I don't know—"

†

"Wow, it's 1987!" Jackson poured some coffee into his mug and leaned against the counter. "You sleep okay?"

Shay smiled. "Yes. Like a baby."

"Good."

Shay felt heat rising on her neck and face as she thought about making love to Talia the night before. They had gone to bed just intending to sleep when Talia rolled over to face her. "I can't stand the thought of not spending the first couple of hours of a brand-new year making love to you," Talia said.

The words had caught Shay totally off guard and she'd grown wet immediately. "What about Jackson?" she'd asked.

Talia rolled over onto Shay and kissed her hard, then whispered, "I bet I can be extremely quiet. How about you?"

And they were. Each time one had been about to call out, the other would cover her mouth and absorb the sound, swallowing it, inhaling it, keeping it hanging in the air like the scent of their sex.

"Shay? Shay?" Jackson interrupted her reverie.

"Oh, sorry. What did you say?" She blushed, and was sure her thoughts of the night before were written all over her face.

"I said Angela's coming by later. She's bringing some black-eyed peas and greens."

Shay squinched up her nose. "Seriously?"

"It's a southern thing," Jackson said.

"Isn't Gish from Chicago? What's with the 'it's a southern thing?'"

Jackson thought about that. "I think you're right but I, for one, will not call her out on that. Besides, she makes killer greens."

"Greens?" Talia asked from the doorway.

"Good morning, sleepyhead," Jackson sang out.

"Good morning. Oh, greens, the smelly stuff you eat on New Year's Day for good luck?" Talia asked.

"You two better eat every last bit on your plates because, no offense, you are not doing so well in the luck department."

Talia nudged Shay. "He sort of has a point but only about the murder stuff. Other than that, I'm feeling pretty damn lucky lately."

Jackson rolled his eyes and Shay smiled.

There was a familiar pattern of knocking on the front door. A key slid into the lock and Jackson helped Angela Gish as she came in with her arms loaded down with a huge pot of food. "Nathan, there's more outside, could you go grab it?"

Jackson headed out and came back with another pot with a pan of corn bread teetering on top. Shay grabbed the pan as it began sliding toward the floor.

Shay noticed Talia sniffing the air with a peculiar look on her face just as Gish noticed too. She held back a chuckle.

"No, you are not already knocking my food without even trying it," Gish said.

"I wouldn't dream of it," Talia responded.

Gish gave her an exaggerated squinty look, then laughed. "Humor me, okay?"

"Okay." Talia nodded toward the bedroom. "I'm going to go take a shower."

"Can you hang on?" Gish asked. "Let me put these pots on the stove to keep everything hot. Then I need to talk to you."

Shay and Talia exchanged glances then went into the den and settled on the sofa.

Gish popped a top on a Coke as she came into the den. "We've had an anonymous call from a woman in New York. She said she's been traveling with Brian and he's crossed into Canada."

"Canada?" Talia asked. "He hates the cold."

"But I guess he'll love the way Canada won't extradite on death penalty cases," Shay said.

"Once a cop, always a cop?" Gish asked Shay, raising an eyebrow. Shay shrugged.

"Do we have anyone trying to substantiate that?" Jackson asked.

"Agents are in New York now."

Shay let out her breath in a rush. She hated the thought of not getting justice for Talia's neighbor's murder, but if Brian was in Canada, at least Talia was safe.

"Don't be getting complacent, now," Gish said to Shay.

"How do you do that?" Shay asked, referring to her knowing what she was thinking.

"I've seen that look on many faces. You still need to eat the good luck black-eyed peas and greens." She headed toward the kitchen. "And you still need to stay put."

"Yes, ma'am," Shay called to her back as she went into the kitchen.

An hour later, Shay was watching with amusement as Talia forced down her good luck meal. Shay had once dated a navy woman from South Carolina and had been made to eat this same meal both New Year's Days they were together. But, she had to admit, Gish's recipe was much better.

"I love the corn bread," Talia said.

Gish laughed. "Just eat a few bites of the peas and greens. I guess you'll be all right since Shay is eating your share as well."

"What I do for you, my love," Shay said, then wondered where the hell the "my love" part came from.

"And don't think for even a minute I don't appreciate it," Talia said.

Jackson nodded his head in their direction and said to Gish, "At least we didn't get stuck with two people who hate each other. Remember that one case last year?"

"Yep. They were so obnoxious I didn't even cook them any greens."

†

"Agents located the young woman who called in the tip about Brian running to Canada. I'm sorry," Jackson glanced at Talia and then looked at Shay. "She was found dead and the coroner thinks she was probably killed right after she made the call to authorities." He leaned against the wall. "We can't say for sure, but it's looking more and more like he's crossed the border into Canada."

"He might never be found up there," Shay said.

"Excuse me," Talia whispered. She walked into the bedroom and shut the door behind her. Poke sat at the door and meowed.

"Come here, sweet boy," Shay said. The cat looked at her but stayed by the door.

Shay closed her eyes for several moments, then opened them and said. "Tell me about the murdered woman."

She forced herself to look at Jackson as he described first the woman, then the crime scene.

"He's a sick dude," Jackson finally added.

"Yes, he is." Shay glanced at the bedroom door. "What now? Do we stay holed up indefinitely? I don't know how much more of this Talia can take. This has been emotionally draining."

"I know it's been hard."

"And I really need to be able to get out there and earn a living again."

He nodded. "I'll talk to the rest of the detail and see what we can come up with."

"Thank you...for everything."

"You are quite welcome." He nodded toward the door to the garage. "I'm going to run on the treadmill for a while since it's cold and drizzly outside."

She nodded, then leaned her head back and closed her eyes. After several moments she felt Talia more than heard her, and opened her eyes. "Hey, sweetheart, you okay?"

Talia sat down beside her on the sofa. Poke jumped up and snuggled between them. They were quiet for several minutes before Talia spoke. "Do you think Brian caught that woman ratting him out and that's why he killed her?"

Shay shrugged. She hoped she was just reading more than what was actually there into Talia's question and that she didn't really think Brian needed a reason to kill someone. "There's no telling."

"What else did Jackson say?" Talia turned slightly on the sofa to face Shay. She stroked the cat as she looked into Shay's eyes.

Shay studied Talia's face. The circles under her eyes were growing darker. Where Shay's nightmares had lessened a little after she told Talia about them, Talia seemed to be growing more and more restless at night. She considered not telling Talia the whole truth, then decided that if she expected total honesty from Talia, she had to reciprocate.

"Shay?"

"He said the scene was identical to your neighbor's. The young woman was found sitting in a recliner with a cord around her neck and she'd been strangled. There was a blanket covering her legs and her hands were in her lap on top of the blanket."

Talia visibly shuddered.

"Sorry," Shay said.

"I can remem—" She hugged her legs against her chest.

"What is it?"

"I can remember one time being home sick. Well, I wasn't sick, I was faking it. Brian knew I wasn't really sick. Hell, he's the one who dared me to lie about it. This was when I was very young and when I first started lying. Anyway, he tucked me in with a blanket around my legs and reminded me that I couldn't change my story under any circumstances. Then he went on to taunt me by asking if I wanted to go out for ice cream or crabbing off the Smith's dock."

"The way those two women were found reminds you of that day?" Shay asked.

"Yeah. What if every little thing he does is about me. What if every death is about me?"

Poke jumped off the sofa.

"It's not your fault," Shay said.

"Not directly."

"Not in *any* way." She slid closer to Talia. "Please don't torture yourself over this. He is playing you and everyone else. Don't let him win by blaming yourself."

Chapter Thirteen

Shay and Talia held hands behind the cat carrier in the backseat of the black sedan. Shay saw the look that passed between Angela Gish and the driver of a matching car they passed a block from Shay's house. Agent Jackson kept his eyes on the side mirror, watching behind them.

"The house has been cleared. Don't be alarmed if at first you notice the presence of a few agents. It's a precautionary measure," Gish said.

Shay looked at Talia, trying to gauge her reaction. Talia nodded toward Gish, then turned to Shay and flashed a smile. Shay had to smile back.

"Shay, you're planning to go back to work at the bar right away?" Jackson asked.

"Yes. I'll be doing security at night and teaching some self-defense on Saturday afternoons." She glanced out the window. "There is still a lot of fear and tension over the murders of Allie and Diane."

"I imagine so," Jackson answered, his voice low.

"Why don't you go ahead and solve that case so we can all relax?"

Jackson turned halfway around to look at Shay. "Hell, why didn't I think of that?"

"Okay, kids," Gish teased. "We're here."

Shay noted her truck in the driveway and how nicely mowed and maintained the yard was. She had a sneaky suspicion Jackson was behind that.

Holding the cat carrier in one hand, Shay pulled a bag from the trunk. The others all grabbed bags and they headed to the front door. Inside Shay could smell the lemony fragrance of a cleaner.

"We didn't want you to have to come home and worry about weeks' worth of dust," Gish said.

"Thank you. Thank you both so much for everything you've done for us since this started," Talia said as she set her bags off to the side.

Shay noticed a catch in Talia's voice. She put down the cat carrier and her bag in the living room and embraced Talia from behind. Talia squeezed her hands.

"So, remember to be vigilant." Gish put her hands on her hips. "Jeffrey being dead doesn't mean every threat has been neutralized. Allie and Diane's murderer is still out there."

Shay stepped away from Talia.

"And Brian could decide to come back into the country. If we hear even the slightest chatter about that possibility, we'll need to secure you again," Jackson added.

Shay saw Talia shudder at the mention of her brother. She wanted to believe that Brian's sense of survival would keep him from returning, but knew that with someone like him there was no way to be certain.

"We'll leave you to it, then," Gish said.

"You have both our phone numbers, and the emergency number. Do not hesitate to call if you need to and we'll keep you informed on any progress in finding the murderer or locating Brian," Jackson said.

As soon as they left, Shay opened the cat carrier. Poke made a beeline for the sliding glass doors where he sat in front of them and meowed.

"Sorry, Poke, being an inside cat didn't kill you at the safe house and it won't kill you here. It may even keep you alive." Shay walked over to him and scooped him up. She stroked him and kissed the top of his head. "Humor me, okay?"

Talia rubbed under his chin.

"You don't mind having an inside cat, do you?" Shay asked Talia.

"No, not at all." She put her hand on the side of Shay's face.

"I really meant it when I said I'd love for you to move in with me."

"I know you did. And I will move in, under one condition."

Shay raised an eyebrow. "I'm listening."

"If it ever gets to the point where you regret asking me to live here, promise you'll tell me. I'd rather find a place of my own and save our relationship than have any cohabitating issues ruin us."

"I promise." She put Poke back on the floor and pulled Talia in for a hug. "I'm so glad to be home and even more glad to be home with you."

"Me too," Talia said into Shay's neck.

†

Talia walked into the bar with Shay and they were immediately engulfed in hugs from Dee, Lana, and Kate.

"Thank God you two are okay," Kate whispered in Talia's ear as they hugged. "It is so good to see you both."

Talia stepped back then as Kate embraced Shay. She thought she might feel a touch of jealousy, but didn't. She realized she felt secure in her relationship with Shay and the thought gave her a warm feeling.

She looked around the bar and felt herself relaxing. It felt good to be out, nice to be out with friends, and terrific to be out with Shay.

Shay went to the far side of the room to see some women and Lana went up to the bar to get a round of drinks, leaving Kate and Talia alone at their table. "So, what's next for you?" Kate asked.

"Shay is talking to a dentist friend of hers about getting me a job. They have a regular dental practice but also make dentures and crowns in their laboratory, and there might be an opening in that area."

"You would want to work in the lab?"

"Oh yeah. That part was always my favorite part of being a dental assistant. I'd rather work with materials than patients any day."

"Then we'll keep fingers crossed that you'll be able to be hired there," Kate said.

"How's school?" Talia asked.

"I'm between semesters right now. Overall it's going very well, but I can't wait to actually see patients one day." Kate played with the empty ashtray. "I'm more sure now than ever before about being a therapist."

"That's great. Any word from your mom?"

"Not yet but I'm not giving up on her coming around."

"Good. You shouldn't give up on her." Talia placed one elbow on the table and leaned slightly forward. "How's April doing?"

"Pretty good. She stayed at the inpatient facility for a couple of weeks but she's home now. She's seeing a therapist and Joey is trying not to work so much."

"So, you think they'll be okay?"

"As a future therapist, I don't know. As her sister, I hope like hell she is," Kate said.

Talia nodded. Weren't their families the strange ones, she thought. Then she took a deep breath and asked the question that kept drifting through her thoughts. "Do you think my brother is a psychopath?" she asked.

"Actually, I think he's a sociopath," Kate said.

"What's the difference?"

"Well, Brian is extremely organized and can be so charming. These characteristics relate more to a sociopath and not a psychopath," Kate said.

"What do you think about me?" Talia looked away as she asked the question.

"You are not your brother, Talia. Period," Kate said. "I'm not saying you aren't charming," she teased, "but you aren't using your charm to manipulate people."

"Hey, how's it going over here?" Lana asked as she placed their drinks on the table and slid into a chair next to Kate.

"Good," they said in unison.

Talia laughed. "It's nice to be out and about." She glanced around the bar until she spotted Shay in the corner talking to Dee.

"We were all really worried," Lana said, also looking at Shay and Dee in the corner. "There was more of a police presence while you two were gone, but the women around here will never trust Officer Parker—or any other straight, male cop—the way they do Shay."

Talia nodded. "I get it."

"When you were hanging out with the feds, did they act like they really wanted to solve Allie and Diane's murders, or do you think they're just going through the motions?" Kate asked.

"I think they really do want to solve this case. I don't know about any of them other than Gish and Jackson, but those two have been really working hard to keep us safe and to find answers," Talia said. She felt confident in the truth of her words.

"Good," Lana said. "Very good."

Shay rejoined their table. She sipped her soda and Talia knew she was still on high alert. She probably would be until the murders were solved and maybe well after that, considering Brian was out there somewhere.

The first notes of a Cyndi Lauper song started and Shay stood. "Dance with me?"

"Yes," Talia said, allowing herself to be led onto the dance floor.

Talia melted into Shay's embrace. As "True Colors" played, Talia felt like she was hearing it for the first time. The pure sound of Cyndi Lauper's voice vibrated through her. Then as the moments ticked by, Talia was no longer hearing the music over the pounding of her heart.

The song ended and they stayed on the dance floor. Shay kissed Talia deeply and Talia knew that nothing else would ever feel as right as that moment, as loving Shay Eliot and being able to show their love to this corner of their world.

†

Two weeks later, Shay opened the door and stepped to the side to let their guests in.

"You look nice," Talia said to Kate as she and Lana came into the house.

"We can only stay a minute." Lana said as she squeezed Kate's hand. "We have some big news and didn't want to tell you over the phone."

"We're meeting Mom and Winston for dinner." Kate's entire face lit up with her words.

"Oh?" Talia smiled. "That's wonderful."

Shay put her arm around Talia's shoulders. "That's great," she added. "When did this happen?"

"Mom called yesterday and we talked for a long time. She said she wanted to see us again and to meet Lana," Kate said.

"I hope the snow stops soon because if it doesn't they might not want to meet us in Emporia," Lana said, massaging Kate's shoulders as she spoke.

"April really wanted to come with us, but she doesn't want to take Joseph out in this weather," Kate said. "She's becoming such a wonderful mother now that she's in counseling."

"That's so terrific," Talia said.

Kate smiled. "I'm so glad April's open to seeing Mom again and I'm thrilled that Mom has reached out to us. I know it's just dinner, but it's a start."

"Baby steps," Shay added.

"Yeah, I know. I'm so happy for these small steps and so grateful for all you two have done to help us work it out. Thank you both."

Talia was about to say it was nothing, but she knew it wasn't, and graciously accepted Kate's words. "You are quite welcome."

"Well," Lana said, "we'd better get going."

"Yeah, we wanted to come by to tell you in person," Kate said.

"Have fun," Talia said.

"Drive safely," Shay added.

They stood at the front door and waved as Kate and Lana pulled away then turned and went inside.

"We did good," Talia said as she hugged Shay.

"You did good," Shay said.

Poke meowed at the back door.

"Are you really going to let him start going out again?" Talia asked.

"Yeah, but he won't go out in the snow."

"Want to go out?" Talia asked him.

"He's faking it," Shay said.

Talia went to the back door and Poke turned and sauntered away, leaving her standing there alone. "He never goes out in the snow?" Talia asked.

"No. But I'm not complaining. I kind of liked him being a totally indoor cat while we were at the safe house. He's too used to going out when he wants to when we're here at home."

"Except when it snows."

"Yep."

Talia followed Shay into the kitchen. When she looked at Shay she couldn't help but smile—a big, contented smile.

Shay stood in front of the kitchen window. "It's really coming down now," she said.

Talia came up behind her and watched as the fat snowflakes floated onto the bushes, the lawn, and the picnic table. "We should go out and play!" Talia bounced up and down on her toes.

Shay laughed. "Okay, but I'm putting on at least two more layers of clothing."

"Okay, you put them on, we'll go out to play, then come in and I'll take them off."

Shay patted her on the cheek. "That's just mean."

"What?"

"Bringing it up and then making me wait."

Talia walked into the hallway and slipped into her coat and gloves. "Come on. The sooner you appease my desire to play outside, the sooner I'll appease your desire to play inside. It is a win for us both, you know."

Shay met Talia in the hallway. "Well, when you put it like that," she said as she raided the coat closet for extra layers.

They finished layering their coats and went outside in the backyard. Talia noted the slight squeak of the snow underfoot. "Hey, let's make snow angels."

Shay gestured to the ground. "After you."

Talia sprawled on her back and started moving her arms and legs to make the snow angel. "Come on, Shay, you do it too."

"If you insist," Shay said. But instead of lying on her back as Talia was, she lowered her body until she was face-to-face on top of Talia. Talia loved the feel of Shay's warmth through her many layers.

"You are my angel," Shay whispered.

Talia kissed her. "Honey?"

"Yes?"

"I'm freezing. I've changed my mind so may we please go play inside now?"

"I thought you'd never ask." Shay got up and pulled Talia to her feet. "Let's go, snow angel."

†

Talia drove her new Ford Ranger across the tunnel to Hampton, on her way to her old apartment in Newport News. The truck was the most inexpensive vehicle she could find and it would be just fine for her. She and Shay had joked about being a two-truck family.

Her lease officially ended later that week and a few boxes of things remained that she wanted to go through. If there was anything left over it could be thrown away. She was sorry she didn't tell Shay she was going to the apartment or at least leave her a note. She knew Shay would want to go with her and Talia didn't want to make a big deal out of it.

Life was getting more and more back to normal. She'd settled in easily with Shay and Poke, and would soon start the job Shay had found for Talia with her dentist friend.

She smiled as she passed the Christmas tree planted in the median that was still adorned in sparkly items for New Year's. So much had changed that it was a relief to see the tree was still there and still being decorated for each new holiday. She would have to ask Kate what she thought of the tree. Since she was usually traveling alone on the interstate, she never thought to ask what anyone else thought of the tree or if they knew who decorated it for each holiday.

She exited the interstate and right away started craving a Slim Jim and Jolt Cola. She made herself show some restraint and went to the apartment first. She stood for several moments in the middle of the living room and noted imprints in the carpet where the furniture she had donated to charity once stood. From the spare room closet, she grabbed the last of her paints and a box of family photos to take with her. What remained she stuffed into two trash bags and carried them to the Dumpster by the mailboxes.

She stood in the parking lot, not wanting to look toward Linda's apartment, but she did look. She noted that the crime scene tape was gone and she assumed someone else was already living there. Life goes on. *How sad.* She adjusted the collar of her coat around her neck, fighting against the chill that had run up and down her spine.

She started the truck and drove to the 7-Eleven. The feeling of being followed was still there and she wondered if it would ever go completely away. She went inside and bought a Slim Jim, potato chips, and a Jolt. As she walked back to the truck, it crossed her mind that she might not ever come to this 7-Eleven again. Her life was in Norfolk now with a new job, new home, and new love. She couldn't help but smile.

She put the key in the door but before she could do more she was grabbed from behind and slammed against the truck door. She sensed the gun more than saw it as Jeffrey Gardner told her to slowly get in the truck and slide across the seat to the passenger side. Her pant leg got caught on the ashtray that was slightly ajar. He punched her in the back and told her to get over. She was finally able to and Jeffrey grabbed the keys from her and started the truck.

"Don't even think about doing anything to piss me off," he growled at her.

"I won't," she gasped. "But, how—?"

"Shut up! I don't want to listen to your stupid questions."

She sat in silence as he drove down the highway with the gun pointed at her side. When he turned onto the parkway, she thought she might throw up.

Jeffrey drove for several miles before he parked her truck at a scenic pull-off and got out, the gun still pointed at Talia. She wasn't sure where she was because they were further down the parkway than she usually went and closer to Jamestown than Yorktown. "Slide over this way and get out," Jeffrey demanded. "And don't make me have to shoot you right here and now."

As she clambered out of the truck, Talia wondered if that meant he preferred to shoot her somewhere else and at some other time.

He shoved her toward the woods. "Move it."

She tripped on a root and lurched forward, falling to her hands and knees. She was thankful for the cushion provided by the blanket of fallen leaves.

"Get up!"

She got back to her feet and he shoved her with his free hand, keeping the gun pointed at her with the other. She had no idea what was in the woods or on the other side because she'd never left the parkway any further than the small beach at Sandy Point.

"Where are we going?"

"Shut up," Jeffrey said.

She managed to keep her footing and after several minutes they came to a small shed. It had double-doors, like a barn or garage. Jeffrey removed an unlocked padlock that secured the doors and pushed her roughly inside. He yanked on an overhead string and a dangling light bulb barely illuminated the room. Talia could make out small engine parts on shelves around the walls. An old wicker chair squatted in the corner, spider webs around its legs.

"Grab that chair from the corner and put it in the middle of the room," he ordered.

She looked at the wicker chair and grew even more scared. She thought about Shay's self-defense class. Avoidance was no longer an option, and neither was drawing attention to them with no one else around. She played Shay's recommendations over and over in her head. She could hear Shay's words, "Go for the eyes, nose, neck, groin…"

Talia took a deep breath, rushed at Jeffrey, viciously shoving the heel of her hand up under his nose, and roaring out as she did so. She ran to the door but it took several jerks to get it open and she almost fell when it did.

Run, she told herself, *run!*

She could hear Jeffrey cussing behind her. She begged her legs to move faster but the sound of his voice got closer and closer. Then she felt his hand on the back of her coat and he jerked her onto the ground.

He rolled her over and straddled her. "You stupid bitch!" he yelled, right before he punched her in the face.

Talia was vaguely aware of being dragged back to the shed. Her vision had started to focus when she realized he was tying her to the unstable wicker chair.

"You stupid bitch," he yelled again. He wiped at his bloodied nose as he paced the short distance from one wall to the other in front of Talia. He held the gun in his right hand. With his left hand he fidgeted with a long knife in a leather sheath attached to his belt.

The longer he went without speaking, the more fearful she grew. Several times she opened her mouth to speak but the look of twisted rage on his face changed her mind. Finally, she couldn't take the silence any longer.

"Who was in the van?" Talia asked, afraid of what the answer might be.

Jeffrey stared at her for a long time. "It wasn't your brother, if that's what you're worried about. It was just some homeless dude."

Relief and anger mixed in her gut. She didn't know how to react to that. "You wanted the cops to think you were dead."

"Yep, and I bet it worked too, didn't it?" He laughed. "I doused the van with gasoline. I learned my lesson from the last time not to use diesel." He wiped his brow. "Who would have known that son-of-a-bitch diesel wouldn't catch fire?"

Talia felt the bile burn her throat as Jeffrey's words sank in. *Last time. Diesel.* She couldn't control the trembling that wracked her body.

Jeffrey let out a growl. "All you had to do was give me the gun. The money would have been nice too but I really just wanted the gun."

"Why was the gun so important?" Talia asked, even though she knew the answer.

"Don't play dumb with me."

"Help me to understand."

"The gun was so important because your asshole brother was going to use it against me."

"How?"

"My prints. After he killed your whore girlfriend with it he tricked me into putting my prints all over it. He would have said that *I* killed that bitch."

Talia opened her mouth, but no words came out. Her breath caught in her chest and she felt like she would suffocate.

"And now, thanks to you, the cops have the gun and will blame me when all I did was help Brian push that bitch's car into the river."

Bernie. Brian killed Bernadette Harris because she'd been with Talia sexually. But how had Brian known? Had he followed them? Had he watched? Talia wanted to throw up.

"That money was for services rendered. I'd earned it moving drugs and helping him get the car into the river. The money was mine and he turned on me, wouldn't give me my stuff." He pulled the knife from the leather sheath on his belt. "You have caused a lot of trouble."

"Jeffrey, I didn't know. I didn't mean to mess you up by giving the gun to the cops."

He slapped her across the face. "And how was I supposed to know there were two other dykes with big hair driving around the parkway in a Honda and fucking women? Huh? How the hell was I supposed to know?"

"What?" Talia asked.

Jeffrey laughed. "You see the absurdity of it too. Crazy, isn't it? I didn't find my stuff in the glove box, but damn it, I would show Brian Lisher not to fuck with me. I would slit his little sister's throat and show him how serious I was."

Talia struggled to breathe.

He leaned in closer to her. "Then on the news it's all about these two *other* dykes. Are you fucking kidding me? I killed the wrong damned dykes!" Spit flew from his mouth and riddled Talia's face.

"No! No! No!" Talia started chanting. "None of this is true. Brian didn't kill Bernie and you didn't kill Allie and Diane. No!"

"The hell we didn't and it was all because Brian couldn't accept the fact that his baby sister is a fucking dyke. See what you did?" He held the knife up to the light and studied it.

†

"There has been a report of a possible abduction at a 7-Eleven in Newport News. The descriptions of the vehicle and woman involved match Talia and her truck."

Shay sat stock-still on the chair across from Agent Gish. All the things she'd been thinking about came rushing to her. The diesel fuel used to douse Allie and Diane, and the fact that Jeffrey Gardner's van used diesel. The leather badge wallet they found stashed in Talia's Honda, and the fact that it looked like Allie and Diane had been pulled over by law enforcement.

"We are looking into possible connections between Brian Lisher, Jeffrey Gardner, and property off the parkway. There's a possible link. Jeffrey's uncle once owned property adjacent to federal lands near Jamestown. We've got folks heading out that way now."

Shay stared straight ahead.

"Shay?" Gish crossed the spaced between them knelt in front of her. "Shay? Look at me. Please."

Shay made eye contact.

"We will find her."

"Losing her will kill me," Shay whispered.

"You aren't going to lose her."

"Angela, you know better than to make promises like that."

She looked away from Shay. "Yes, I do know better but that doesn't mean I'm not going to say it anyway. If I say it out loud, maybe..."

"Yeah, maybe." Shay nodded her head. "What can I do now to help?"

"Nothing. Stay put."

"Oh, you know I can't—"

"Yes you can, and you will. I am tasked with keeping you here and out of the way. Understand?"

†

Talia's sobs grew faster, more intense. "No. You're crazy. You're making all of this up."

"Yeah? Just ask your cop buddies about the matchbook shoved down the throat of the one I thought was you. Oh, wait, you can't ask them because you are dead." He pressed the knife against her neck and she gasped.

"Please don't."

"Should I slit your throat like the others? Or should I gut you? Yeah, I could cut you from one end to the other—gut you like an animal. Wouldn't that be something for Brian to see?"

"Please—"

"I'd like to gut your dyke girlfriend as well. I should have taken care of her after we left the parkway that night she got the drop on me. But I'll let Brian have her."

Talia jumped when the door to the shed exploded. Brian stood among the splintered wood with a pistol raised and pointed at Jeffrey. "You really shouldn't have messed with my sister, dude," Brian said, pulling the trigger and shooting Jeffrey twice in the chest.

Talia sat, motionless, still tied to the chair, horrified as she stared at Jeffrey's still twitching body and terrified of what her brother might do.

"Tali-ho! Look at you, sis, you don't look so great."

"Brian—"

"Surprise! You can thank me later." He bent over to untie her ankles then paused before untying her hands. "Behave. I don't want to have to hurt you, but I will."

She nodded her head. "How did you find me?"

"Jeff and I used to hang out here back in the good old days when we moved some pretty good quantities of pot and coke." He studied her. "Have you learned to drive a stick since I've been gone?"

"What? No."

"Too bad. My new girlfriend up in New York let me borrow her car but it's a stick. Where are the keys to that truck?"

"In his pocket." She nodded her head toward Jeffrey's bloodied body.

"Get them."

She only hesitated a moment, then went through Jeffrey's pockets until she found her truck keys.

"Where's the Honda? I can't believe you don't have my Honda." His voice was whiny and he gave her a look of disgust. "Let's go." He gestured toward the splintered door with the gun. "Come on."

†

As Talia drove her truck along Route 17 she glanced at the gun resting on her brother's lap. They passed her usual Exxon station then passed her Taco Bell. They passed, and were passed by, dozens of cars, all with people oblivious to what was happening in the nondescript Ford Ranger.

"I am dead serious, Tali. You take me to your girlfriend now or I will kill you and still find her. I promise I will kill her gently, but if you fuck this up for me, when I do kill her, it will be torturous for her. Understand?"

She nodded her head. "Yeah, I understand," she whispered. "Why are you doing this?"

"She has ruined you and she needs to pay for that," Brian said, his manner very matter-of-fact.

"She hasn't ruined—"

"Shut up," he said. "I can't believe you're a fucking dyke."

"Why does that bother you so much? I don't understand. Who I sleep with doesn't hurt you in any way."

"Shut up!" He raised his fist as if to strike her, but then lowered it into his lap, resting his clenched hand by the one holding the gun.

Talia felt tears burn her cheeks.

"Do you remember Jodie Summers?" Brian asked.

"Jodie Summers? Didn't she move away when you were in the sixth grade?"

"I was madly in love with Jodie. Do you know why they moved away?" He didn't wait for her to answer the question. "Jodie's mom turned into a dyke and hooked up with this— this—thing named Mary Beth. I asked Jodie if we could still go steady after she moved and she told me no, that she couldn't be my girlfriend because she was going to be a lesbian just like her mom."

193

"She was a kid and probably didn't even know what that meant. Not that it should matter. It's none of anyone's business if Jodie and her mom were lesbians," Talia said.

"I should find them and see if Jodie did turn into a lesbian."

"And then do what, Brian?"

"Kill her, of course." He shot her a look of disgust. "And don't think for a moment that I won't kill you just because you're my sister."

She turned to look at him then.

"Besides, if you do as you're told and bring me to Shay, not only will I let you live but I will reward you." When she didn't respond to that, he went on. "Take me to your girlfriend and I will tell you the truth about what happened to Dad."

She gasped.

"If you don't behave, you will never know the truth. I know how much you want to know if you let him die that day."

"What?"

"Drive. Behave. Then you'll know."

When she glanced in the rearview mirror, a dark sedan caught her eye. She had seen so many of the agents' cars that she immediately recognized it as one. She looked away quickly, not wanting to draw Brian's attention to the car tailing them.

She looked over at her brother and his smile sent a chill right through her.

He nodded toward the gun in his lap. "You will behave, right?"

"Yes, Brian, I will behave," she answered.

"I will not hesitate to kill you, relative or not." He sat in silence for several minutes then said, "Oh, the suspense must be killing you." He laughed. "I will give you an early reward and tell you about Dad so that you don't think for even a moment that I won't kill you if you don't do as I say."

She struggled to swallow past the boulder that had formed in her throat.

"Oh, little sister, Dad was so pissed at you. He was talking about sending you away and I told him he would regret it, but he blew me off. So I spiked his morning coffee and waited for him to get into the bath. Once the sleeping pills kicked in, it took no effort at all to hold him under the water."

Her stomach roiled. Brian had drugged their father, and then drowned him. He was a monster even back then. How did she not see that? What in the hell did it say about her that she couldn't see what a dangerous person her brother was? Her chest ached. She felt like her heart would implode right then and there.

"And then I saw you go into the bathroom. When you went back to bed without saying a word, I was so proud of you. I can guess you have felt guilt over that for years. You feel guilt because you are weak."

She stared straight ahead. Apparently he could have killed any one of them at any time. She thought about the blackberries. When she was quite young she loved blackberries. They grew all over the neighborhood, a briar patch here, a patch there and she could eat them by the quart. Until the day Brian had brought her to a patch down the road and showed her how the leaves looked different—hell, she didn't know one leaf from another—and explained to her that those berries were poisonous. Then he lowered his voice and told her he'd seen their mother picking them and he figured she was going to try to poison them. It was ten years before Talia could eat blackberries again. It took her friend, Debbie, laughing at her when Talia had mentioned the poisonous form of the berries to drive Talia to the library to search for the truth. She never told Brian she knew and she never let him see her eat the berries.

"So, that is my present to you. The truth. The bastard was gone long before you stumbled upon his dead ass in the tub." He looked at her. "Now, get on 134."

She merged easily onto the ramp that would lead them to the road that would take them to the interstate. She noted the Dairy Queen closed for the winter and glanced again in the mirror and was relieved when she saw the sedan was still behind them. It appeared that an unmarked county car had also fallen into line. Her heart started pounding.

"Is this the fastest this crap truck can move?" Brian asked.

She accelerated slightly. Then it occurred to her that she really didn't want to get onto the interstate. The idea of taking him one step closer to where Shay lived almost overwhelmed her. Making up her mind, she glanced one last time in the mirror, trying to will the agent in the sedan to read her mind. She focused on a tree on the right side of the road, jerked the wheel sharply, and ran the truck into that tree. She'd braced herself, but still felt the pain of impact. She could see Brian lurch forward, hitting the windshield.

The impact of her chest with the steering wheel made her breaths painful, but she ignored that and pushed open the truck's door. She ran as fast as she could toward the nearest driveway.

Behind her, a dozen voices were yelling at Brian to drop the gun.

Talia tripped and fell to the ground then scrambled on her hands and knees across the gravel shoulder of the road, only half aware of the little rocks cutting into the palms of her hands.

"Tali!" Brian called out.

She couldn't stop herself from looking back at him and was amazed to see the number of police cars that had seemingly come out of nowhere.

Brian stood outside of the truck, blood running down the side of his face. He leveled the gun at her. "I love you to death, kiddo."

She saw the decision in his eyes a split second before realizing he'd pulled the trigger. Pain exploded in her shoulder and, as she was thrown backward by the force of the bullet, she saw Brian jerk and contort as a barrage of bullets hit him.

†

Shay squeezed Talia's hand when she opened her eyes. "Hey, look who's awake."

"Hi," Talia said, her voice raspy. She tried to sit up. "Ouch," she said before settling back on the bed.

"The doctor said the surgery went great. Your shoulder should heal fine and be as good as new." She studied Talia's face, wondering how long it would take for her to ask about her brother.

"I'm starving."

"Want me to see if the nurse will bring you some ice chips or Jell-O?"

"How about some Taco Bell?" Talia asked.

"I don't think that will go over so well yet." She leaned closer. "I'm so glad you are okay."

Talia smiled. "I'll believe you when you sneak in a burrito for me, or, better yet, kiss me."

Now Shay smiled. "I can definitely do the kiss thing." She leaned into Talia and kissed her gently on the lips.

The next morning, Shay was back at Talia's side when she awoke. "Still here?" Talia whispered.

"Where else would I be?" Shay asked.

"The FBI will want my statement," Talia said.

"When you're ready."

"Can you get me some paper and a pen?" Talia asked. "I keep thinking about a poem I want to write before it disappears."

"Sure." Shay went out into the hallway and returned with pen and paper. "Here you go."

"Thanks." Talia tucked it beside her leg, then turned to Shay. "So, Shay? I was wondering…"

Shay knew the question before it was asked.

"Did Brian survive?"

"No, Talia. No, he didn't." Shay thought about saying she was sorry, but that would have been a lie and she couldn't lie to Talia and expect the truth from her in return.

"He killed my father," Talia said. "That's all I want to ever say about it. But there it is. Probably the only truthful thing Brian has ever said to me."

"I'm sorry, Talia. I'm sorry about your father and all the guilt you had to endure over the years. All for nothing." Shay forced herself to stop talking. It wouldn't help Talia for Shay to get angry.

Shay walked to the window as Talia jotted down some words. She wanted to give Talia some privacy while writing. She stared down into the parking lot and was almost overtaken by emotion at the thought of how badly things could have turned out. She forced those thoughts away.

"Shay, will you come back?" Talia asked. Talia handed her the paper.

"May I read it?" Shay asked.

"Yes." Talia turned slightly away then.

Shay read out loud, in a whisper:

"Defined by the other,
seasoned to embrace that life.
Lizard's tongue tasting the lies in the air.
But love empowers, so I dart away,
leaving behind my tail
with the tar-blisters and thorns.
I take with me only
the blackberries,
honeysuckle,
and your vanilla."

Shay swiped at a tear as Talia turned back to look at her. "I love it."

Talia squeezed Shay's hand. She was quiet for several minutes before she spoke. "I can trust so few memories from growing up. There is what I think happened, what Brian said happened, and what really did happen. But once it's been colored with lies it's almost impossible to know the truth," Talia said.

Shay nodded and leaned closer. "There is one truth I want you to know always. I love you."

"I love you too," Talia responded. "And no words out of my mouth have ever been more honest than that."

23 Miles

Author's Afterword

I graduated from York High School in 1982. While in high school, I spent my share of time on the Colonial Parkway, parking and partying. By 1983 I had come out and was mostly hanging out in Norfolk, enjoying the lesbian scene there.

In October of 1986, the bodies of Cathleen Thomas and Rebecca Ann Dowski were found in Thomas's Honda Civic on the Colonial Parkway. The women had been brutally murdered. Their throats were slashed and there was evidence of strangulation and ligature marks. They were the first of four double-murders in what would become known as the Colonial Parkway Murders, even though only four of the eight murders presumably occurred on the actual parkway.

In September of 1987, David Knobling and Robin Edwards were found murdered in the Ragged Island Wildlife Refuge. David's truck was found first then days later, their bodies. They had been shot.

Then on April 9, 1988, the other event on the parkway occurred. Richard "Keith" Call's car was found abandoned on the parkway. Both his driver's door and glove box were open. Personal items were found in the car, but there was no sign of Call or his passenger. Keith Call and Cassandra Hailey were missing. Never found, they are presumed dead.

Labor Day weekend, 1989, Daniel Lauer's car was found abandoned at a rest area between Richmond and Williamsburg. In October of that year, the bodies of Daniel and Annamaria Phelps were found by hunters in the woods near that rest area.

All four of these double-murders resembled traffic stops in some way, all showed limited amounts of struggle (Cathy Thomas is the only one who seems to have resisted), and all were couples found in relatively remote areas.

But there were differences too, most notably the weapons and methods used.

The Thomas and Dowski murders more closely resemble a double-murder that happened ten years later in Shenandoah National Park. Julie Williams and Lollie Winans were murdered on another holiday weekend, Memorial Day, in 1996. Both of these cases involved women in remote areas, all had their throats slashed, and all happened on National Park Service property.

These murders had a profound effect on both my hometown community in York County and my new stomping grounds in Norfolk. The sheer brutality of the Thomas and Dowski murders shocked the quiet, historical county where my friends and I walked alone at night without fear and our neighbors weren't concerned with locking their front doors. As for my community in Norfolk—we had lost two of our own in a most heinous way and we were scared.

There are many theories, of course I have my own, but for this book I wanted to take the first double-murder and fictionalize it, and use this fictional story to show how violent crimes affect so many people. And of course, there is always my hope that maybe someone will pick up this book one day, read it, and have a memory come to them, and maybe it will be just the right piece of information to move the investigation forward.

I also hope this serves as a call to action. Both the FBI and the NPS had their hands on the Thomas/Dowski and Call/Hailey investigations (and later the Winans/Williams case in Shenandoah National Park). There is a lot of talk that both investigative forces made mistakes. Now might be a good time to look more thoroughly into these cases and, using today's forensics and technologies, find a way to give the families of these victims some answers, closure, and justice.

If you, the reader, know anything about activities on or around the parkway—however small or seemingly inconsequential—please come forward. You might have the key to solving one or all of these crimes and not even know it.

You can call the FBI at 757-455-0100 or email Colonial_Parkway_Murders@ic.fbi.gov.

If you prefer, you can also email the author at 23Miles.Tips@gmail.com.

About the Author

Renee MacKenzie

As a Navy brat, Renee lived on three continents before her family settled in Virginia. She currently resides in Southwest Florida with her partner, Pam, and their poodle, Sabrina. Renee works and plays in the swamp, where she enjoys wildlife photography, kayaking, and hiking. Even though Renee has been paid to do all sorts of jobs, ranging from dental assistant to bartender, data entry clerk to maintenance worker, and field sampler to pet-sitter, she insists she's only had one job—writer—and all the rest has just been research.

Other Books from Affinity eBook Press

Confined Spaces—Renee MacKenzie Andie Waters spends her days pulling waste samples for environmental testing and at night, she tends bar at The Cave, a popular hangout for straights in a small Georgia town. Serial monogamy has grown stale for her, so she's content working to pay off her debts and hanging out with her old hound dog. Or so she thinks, until a beautiful lesbian drops by The Cave. Andie suspects her involvement with the woman will be only temporary. Little does she know no part of her life will be left untouched. Kara Travis likewise anticipates nothing more than a brief fling upon meeting Andie, especially given her reputation as both a personal ice princess and a corporate hatchet wielder for Royal Environmental. What luck to find a hot lesbian bartender in nowhere rural Georgia. Andie and Kara spend a passionate weekend together and find that their notions of no strings attached are far from accurate. Their supposed short-term ideal diversion of a commitment-free romp hits a major complication when they come face-to-face with one another at Royal Environmental's offices Monday morning. While carrying out her duties, Kara discovers crimes being committed by and against Royal Environmental employees. Will Kara be forced to shut down the Georgia Division of the company? If she does, Andie will lose her job. Worse yet, Kara may lose Andie before she's really even sure she's got her. Corporate politics, complicated romance, and long distances conspire to keep Andie and Kara all boxed in. Can love triumph despite the Confined Spaces?

Reece's Star—TJ Vertigo Reece Corbett watches over the dancers in her gentleman's club with the blue, razor-sharp eyes of The Animal. Few know that resting comfortably in her office is her newest love, a tiny MinPin named Smudge. What happened to The Animal, known for her rapacious appetite for women and danger? Faith Ashford is what happened to The Animal. Faith and Reece have been together a while now and they have settled into something resembling domestic bliss. This bliss alarms Reece. It's one thing for Faith to see her softer side, that's vulnerability enough, but to let her friends see it...no. Not the best plan. Under Faith's guiding, loving hand, will Reece successfully traverse the rocky road of emotion and embrace the positive changes in her life? Or will she panic and be unable to control that Animal part of herself? Will she take that next step to declare herself fully capable of love and devotion? This third installment in the popular series that began with *Private Dancer* continues the passionate and often hilarious romance of Reece and Faith as they both grow in love and in trust.

Flight—Renee MacKenzie It's 1983 and Kate Hunter is a student at a small, private college in Virginia. When Lana coaxes her onto the back of her beat-up scooter one night, Kate's education starts to encompass more than just her pre-vet studies. Kate has always done as expected of her, so when she starts staying away from home on weekends to spend time with her new lover it's way out of character for her. Lana is secretive, but Kate accepts things as they are and gives Lana her space. When she feels the sting of betrayal, will she be able to continue giving Lana her privacy? Kate's sister April is a high school student playing with fire as she parties with her older boyfriend, Boyd. After finding someone overdosed the morning after a big party, April grows weary of all the drugs and alcohol. Will she be able to convince Boyd that they should slow down? Will she be able to pull it together before it's too late? Kate and April are forced to face up to events from their younger years, their mother's desertion, and their long-deteriorating relationship with one another. Some lives will be lost and others changed forever when the sisters' lives intersect. Will they be consumed by the wreckage, or will they be able to pick themselves up and take flight?

Reflected Passion—Erica Lawson   Where passion, reality, and destiny combine.
Dale Wincott is a 27-year-old woman born into Bostonian wealth and groomed to marry into the social hierarchy. Her mother is a hard-hearted society matriarch, but her father feels for his daughter and helps Dale find a life on her own as a furniture restorer. Françoise Marie Aurélie de Villerey is a 28-year-old Countess, born into the French aristocracy and forced to marry a count much older than herself. For ten years, she was his trophy wife, forced to endure his perverted desires, until the day he finally died. He had broken her emotionally and she no longer cared for what life had to offer, slipping from one sexual partner to another as often as she changed her clothes. Until...that one night when Françoise looked up during a sexual encounter and saw Dale watching her from the mirror. A veritable angel, full of innocence and curiosity, who touched her very soul. Through the mirror, Françoise embraces life anew, while for Dale it is a powerful awakening, forcing her to discover not only her sensual nature, but the inner strength she possesses.

PUNK AND ZEN Part. 2: The ReMaster (Deep DJ Cut)—JD Glass Remixed, remade, and relaunched, because the someday Nina's been working so hard for is *now*, and all the work she's done has brought her here: her first band, her first tour, and her first trip to Europe, all at the same time. But these baby steps to success don't come without a price, because there are other firsts, as well: first true heartbreak, first time really alone and oh-so-far from anyone or anything she knows... And when the one who created the heartbreak shows up with the one who promised forever, here comes another first: does she choose between them, does she cut them both out or does she go within and decide...differently? Punk And Zen Part 2: The ReMaster (Deep DJ Cut): cutting down to bone.

The One—JM Dragon Phil (Philomena) Casters loves her work as a pilot, above everything else in her life except Ming, her married lover. Phil needs to enhance her status in the community before asking Ming to leave behind her wealthy husband. Rosa Moran is a teacher raised by missionaries in China after the death of her parents. She loves the country of her birth and the people. Her English grandfather desperately wants her to live with him to atone for the guilt he feels about the death of her parents. He sends her a letter requesting her to come home. When Phil flies to the mission to deliver the letter to Rosa, neither can envisage the chain of events about to take place. It starts as a collaboration to save four children, leading them to the surreal private paradise of Langshow. Could this be the perfect place for the children and Rosa to settle? Phil is not so sure. Chang, an old friend from Rosa's childhood lives in Langshow and makes no bones about the fact that he wants Rosa. All thoughts of Ming disappear as Phil tries to fight her attraction to Rosa. However there is the little matter of an innocent misunderstanding—Rosa thinks Phil is a man. *The One* is a romance with everything, love, intrigue, misunderstandings with a happy conclusion—the only question—who gets the girl?

The Chronicles of Ratha: Book 2 A Lion Among the Lambs—Erica Lawson   It has been three years since Jordana Laren's path first crossed the Noorthi's—three years since she's had a drink, had sex and a life of her own. Her only excitement has been spent keeping up with her two-year-old daughter, Rice, who is definitely a chip off the old block. All has been peaceful until one of the colonists becomes sick. Bad news shifts to worse news when the disease spreads through their community. Unable to get proper medicine, Jordana is forced to rely on the Noorthi healers to come up with a cure. Soon the herbs run out, leaving her with no choice but to search for more on the Noorthi home planet. What is supposed to be a simple pick-up flight turns into a nightmare. Can Jordana believe in herself like her Noorthi sisters do? Only then can she fulfill her destiny as The Chosen One. Follow the colorful cast of characters in this action-packed adventure sequel as they traverse the galaxy. Of course, nothing ever goes smoothly when Jordana is involved.

Cowgirl Up—Ali Spooner   When the new ranch hand, Coal Bryan, arrives at the MC2, the last thing she's looking for is love. Her co-workers are surprised when Coal turns out to be female. Coal, used to the reaction, quickly earns the respect of the crew with her work ethic and skill with horses. Coal uses the strenuous work and friendship of the ranch hands to try and forget her broken past. Melissa Conway, owner of MC2, offers Coal a place to live in her home. They both are shocked to find they are linked in a way neither of them imagined. Mary Leah, Melissa's sister, arrives at the ranch to recover from a recent tragedy. The attraction between Mary Leah and Coal is instant and mutual. Can the three women survive their personal dilemmas? The love and friendship they develop certainly helps but will it be enough to bring them together. Ride along with the MC2, for boot scootin', butt kickin', dirt eatin', rodeo adventures, with a love story thrown into the mix.

If I Were a Boy—Erin O'Reilly Katie McGuire appears to have it all. A devoted husband, a job she loved, and a comfortable lifestyle. Helen Swenson is a successful financial director of a prominent investment firm, with an unfaithful husband and few friends. Their husbands' annual trip to Padre Island National Seashore to reunite with their air force pilot squad becomes a pivotal point for the two women. Their lives take on a completely new meaning when an undeniable magnetism between them draws them together. Passion and secrecy becomes the norm, as they have no choice but to succumb to their attraction. Can the vacation love affair continue? When they leave for their respective homes, will they regret what happened? Life is not that easy to change and the people around them are the hardest to convince. There is no more powerful motivation than love. Except hate and there are plenty of people who want to see their relationship destroyed. Will Katie and Helen be able to make a life together work or succumb to doubts and the pressures of family? This story will fill you with the thrill of passion and the tenderness of love.

Nesting—Renee MacKenzie Macy Stokes, a divorced mother who is struggling with her sexual identity, jumps at a once-in-a-lifetime opportunity to help her friends. She doesn't foresee it will put her in jeopardy of losing her son,

Jeremiah. Fresh out of high school, Cam Webber travels to Augusta, Georgia, to reconcile with her aunt. When she learns that's impossible, she determines to gain acceptance from her aunt's partner, Sharon. Meanwhile, Cam sets her sights on Macy, but Macy has other ideas. Kenny Brewer is a good old boy who loves his wife, Dorianne, even when he thinks she's gone totally off her rocker. Dorianne gets it in her head that a local woman is her long-lost half-sister. But soon, her obsession with that is eclipsed by medical problems that involve them all. Set in Augusta, Georgia, *Nesting* explores the age-old issues of guilt, regret, and redemption, and the part they play in driving people to create and protect family—at any cost.

Reece's Faith—TJ Vertigo   In the return of the main characters from the bestselling novel *Private Dancer*, we see the blossoming relationship of bar owner, Reece Corbett and actress, Faith Ashford. The two women explore new, uncertain territory together, using sexual intimacy as a glue of comfort, helping them become strong and whole. A trusting Reece shares with Faith the sordid tale of how she became *The Animal* and Faith finds herself newly empowered by Reece's ongoing trust and support. Jealousy arises when Faith has to kiss a man on her TV show and two amorous women stalk Reece. When Faith is outed on her television show, things get crazy. With the arrival of her parents on the scene, the craziness escalates. As Faith tries to justify her lifestyle and defend her love for Reece, she discovers that nothing about her parents is as she once believed. This not-to-be-missed passionate and erotic romance will have you begging for more.

Starting Over—Jen Silver   Ellie Winters, a successful potter, is living on a remote hilltop farm inherited from her

210

parents. Her well-ordered life is shaken apart when her past meets her present. Robin Fanshawe, Ellie's philandering long-term lover, has a fragile truce with Ellie. The arrival of women from Robin's present threatens to break that tentative pact. Charming Dr. Kathryn Moss, an archaeologist and an old lover of Ellie's, arrives on the farm searching for a new site to dig. When she discovers a previously unknown Roman settlement and ancient burial site on Ellie's farm, Ellie allows her to start an archaeological dig of the area. Will Ellie also allow the rekindling of an old romance or will she stay with Robin? Can that long-term relationship, albeit tentative, recover from this collision or will an old romance trump everything she knows? Will Robin, seeing the interaction between Ellie and Kathryn, leave her womanizing ways behind? Will she take a chance on giving herself wholly to the woman she loves? These questions and the mystery of whose royal resting place is disturbed at Starling Hill are answered in this classic romance of simmering passions, anguished loss, and the wonder of love.

Twisted Lives—Ali Spooner A twist of fate as she flees the control of an abusive husband leaves Bet and her daughter Kylie stranded at the entrance of the home of Alex Graves. When custom homebuilder Alex arrives to find steam boiling from Bet's car and a beautiful child asleep in the passenger seat, her heart goes out to them. Alex offers shelter to the pair, setting off a chain of events that bring both mother and daughter close to her heart and danger to her door. A heartwarming story of true love that will keep you smiling long after you've finished the book.

Malodorous—Del Robertson Sequel to My Fair Maiden Something in Fairhaven stinks. Other than the mutton stew, that is. Gwen thought life after being a virgin sacrifice would be a bed of roses. Bodhi was just looking for a wench to bed. Neither less-than-dashing hero nor not-quite-so-pure maiden imagined they would meet again, much less be trapped together in a city the likes of the ill-named Fairhaven. There's a killer on the loose. Fairhaven's on lockdown, its citizens fearful for their lives. The local guards are corrupt. And, Bodhi's been accused of murder…

Desert Blooms—Dannie Marsden Luce's story continues in DESERT BLOOMS… When we last met Luce Velazquez in Desert Heat, she went through hell and back to salvage her soul and reputation. Hoping to get her life back on track with lover Beth Ryan, a woman who understands her pain and can relate on every level. Instead, Luce is in the hospital, and Beth in protective custody. Jessica Sullivan, Luce's friend and ex, has big doubts about the sincerity of Beth's love, and is in no hurry to release her from custody. Can Luce's new found happiness last, or is Jessica correct in her doubts? A heart-stopping romance that will fill you with the wonder of friendship, anger of betrayal, and the everlasting vision of love.

Cold and Lonely, Lovely Work of Art—S. Anne Gardner Two worlds clash one day and neither will ever be quite the same again. Barbara comes from a world of safety but filled with lies. Taya comes from a world of darkness and violence. From the bowels of an underworld filled with the drug of choice, the white, and the trade of human flesh comes 'Black Angel.' She is the personification of death in the pens and all tremble with the mere mention of her name. Barbara's world is spinning off its axis with the deception of a life filled with lies and the uncertainty of all that she has known. One afternoon she crosses into a foreign domain and her world is never the same again. Two completely different women from utterly different worlds clash and the fusion is explosive. Passion, sex, violence, vice, beauty, love...

HER—Lisa Ron Fox has been looking for that one person who will make her feel complete—her perfect match. Together with her friends, Megan and Tree, Fox continues her quest while dodging exes and clingers, laughing a lot along the way. When she meets Madeline, she instantly knows that she has found HER. Madeline has her own problems—notably a domineering husband. Can Fox win her heart? Can they make a life together? This story will make you laugh, cry, and hold your breath as the story unfolds. With the right person love can conquer all.

Bayou Justice—Ali Spooner Hell hath no fury like a woman scorned. When Kara, Sasha's new lover is taken hostage as a diversionary tactic to allow the drug dealing Bellfontaine brothers to escape justice, Sasha springs into action. Kara is released physically unharmed, however her emotions and budding career in the District Attorney's office are left in shambles when she is held to blame for their release, Appalled by the failure of the criminal justice system, Sasha exacts her own brand of justice for the acts committed against her lover. From the Bayous of Louisiana to the jungles of South America, Sasha plots her revenge.

Letting Go—JM Dragon A failed relationship puts Stella Hawk's life on the brink of chaos. When her grandmother falls gravely ill in Ashville, Stella ends her army career to take care of the woman during her last weeks. Little does she know that an old army comrade, socialite Reggie Stocton, whose family owns the local newspaper, also lives in Ashville. Will she allow herself to accept Reggie's help to turn her life around and let go of the past? This is a journey where both women re-evaluate what they want out of life. Will that path lead to happiness or to a parting of the ways?

E-Books, Print, Free e-books

Visit our website for more publications available online.

www.affinityebooks.com

Published by Affinity E-Book Press NZ LTD
Canterbury, New Zealand

Registered Company 2517228